THE
WIND GATE

She was angry with these kids, they were wasting her time with their hide-and-seek. Little boys' games . . . It wasn't until she reached the water, and they'd not found Howard, that she felt the first chill of unease. It wasn't till the great splash echoed round the quarry walls, echoed and echoed, and grey ripples started lapping at her feet, that she was afraid.

THE
WIND
GATE

Philip Gross

■SCHOLASTIC

Scholastic Children's Books,
7–9 Pratt Street, London NW1 0AE, UK
a division of Scholastic Publications Ltd
London ~ New York ~ Toronto ~ Sydney ~ Auckland

Published in the UK by Scholastic Publications Ltd, 1995

ISBN 0 590 54191 9

Typeset by DP Photosetting, Aylesbury, Bucks
Printed in England by Clays Ltd, St Ives plc

10 9 8 7 6 5 4 3 2 1

Almost all the places in this story are real, but the names and the distances between them have been changed. You can walk Howard's journey for yourself . . . but use a map.

1.

"It happens sudden... When you're not expecting. One moment you're driving along, look, enjoying the view. Tum-ti-tum..."

From where Howard and Steve were sitting, Dunk's thick little glasses were reflections of the sky. He turned his head slightly, right to left and back again, and he steered an imaginary wheel. His stubbled chin creased in a grin.

It's true what they say, thought Howard. He's cracked.

"Tum-ti-tum," hummed Dunk, enjoying the view. There wasn't a view, of course – just the back of the sports hut and a dusty bramble hedge. That was why they were there, Steve and Howard – out of sight, out of mind, while the others got put through their paces in the 500 metres and the long jump. As for Dunk, well, he came with the place. You could usually see him pushing his huge iron roller up and down. Up and down. He had to be stupid. Who would want a job like that? Who'd want to be assistant groundsman on a playing field where kids laughed behind your back, day after day?

"Tum-ti-tum. And then – all of a sudden..." He leaned towards them. "They GETS you! From behind. Always from behind, it is, else you'd see them coming, wouldn't you?"

"What?" said Steve. "What gets you?"

"The Hands, of course! Gurt things with hair all down the back and nails like ... nails like this!" He held up the rusty chisel he'd been using to scrape things off the roller – dead grass, mushed snails, flakes of rust. "The Hairy Hands," said Dunk. "Everybody knows about he."

"I don't," said Steve.

"That's cause you don't come from round here. I knows that." Dunk tapped his nose. "The way you speaks. You're from Lunnon."

How old was Dunk? Thirty? Older? Hard to tell. He talked like a first year just come up from primary school . . . except that he was twice that size, with bristles on his chin and a creased sort of look all over. There was something about the way he walked and stood – he often just *stood* – that said: peculiar. He was the kind of person parents told you not to make remarks about. You were not to say: dim, dur-brain, thick.

So when Dunk came round the hut and found them sitting there, anyone else would have sniggered and run off. Not Steve. He could talk to anybody, any age. He struck up a conversation. Where are you from? Where's that? Dartmoor? What's it like? Next moment, Dunk was squatting by his roller, telling them stories of the moor.

"What happens then?" said Steve. "After it gets you?"

Dunk shook his head. "How do I know? You'd be dead when they find you."

"Just a moment . . ." Howard started. If the victims were dead when they found them, how did anybody know about the Hands? "Surely . . . Yaagh!" Two claw-like hands clapped over Howard's eyes from behind, and as he yelped and rolled away there was Steve behind him, laughing. Howard blushed, a strawberry-mousse kind of pink. That was him all over.

Easily embarrassed wasn't the word for it. If there was an Embarrassment Olympics, Howard could blush for England.

He didn't quite know how it had happened, him and Steve being friends, if that was what they were. Like everyone else, Howard had noticed when this new kid turned up with longer-than-the-school-likes hair and Walkman plugged in all the time. Steve made no effort to make friends. He seemed quite content in there, his head rattling with heavy metal. He made no effort to join groups or gangs, as if he didn't care. Nobody liked that, not the other kids or the teachers. Sometimes he bothered with a school uniform sweater, sometimes not. Then he wore a T-shirt saying SKELETON CRUE in blood-splatter red above a skull with a horned Viking helmet and a hollow grin.

He talked sort of casual, quietly and quick, with a hint of the States in it somewhere. Not posh, but he made the Plymouth kids around him sound like yokels. No one liked that, either. And now somehow Howard was his friend.

It happened like this. One evening, up the little rat-run alley by the school gates, a bunch of the usual kids were hanging round, leaning on the walls, blocking most of the way. Howard knew, the way they looked at him, that they were going to jostle him a bit, maybe call a few names – nothing really vicious, just what he was used to. As the first one stuck a grubby Nike out in his way, there was Steve's voice behind him. "Leave my friend alone."

The others gawped. What, *him?* you could hear them thinking, but they didn't say. That was the other thing about Steve. He wasn't soft. You wouldn't think it, with his smooth kid-brother face. When his hair flopped forward you could almost take him for a girl. Someone had said that once, early on, and woken up in hospital.

Howard gawped too. What, *me?* Steve had never spoken to him before.

"Come on," Steve said, and together they walked between the double file of kids, who kept their sneers on . . . but didn't move or breathe.

"Thanks," said Howard, once they were well out of sight. Steve shrugged. "They're all mouth," he said. "You've got to show them." And he sort of yawned. Thinking back later, Howard wondered if that could be it. Steve didn't rate anybody in this place. Helping another odd one out, especially one as helpless as Howard . . . well, it passed the time.

Put it another way: could it be that Steve had done it because he was bored?

But they were friends now. Sort of.

Out beyond the sports hut Mr Fairbairn's voice barked on: "Go on! Push yourselves! Make it hurt!" He was one of those games teachers who look as if they're made from knotted string, and wear shorts in December. Every school's got one, Steve said casually. He'd been in plenty, he should know. The more it hurt, the more they liked it, and he wasn't going to give Mr Fairbairn the satisfaction.

"Tell us another one," he said to Dunk.

" 'Taint a story," the assistant groundsman said, warily. "There really is a Hands."

"What about the Flip Flop?" said Howard and immediately went pink. He had heard some of the boys who were Scouts, who'd been out camping on the moors, say something, but they could have been having him on.

"Oh, that one," said Dunk. He nodded slowly. "You don't want to run into he."

"It's real then, is it?" said Howard. Dunk gave a glance at Steve. It was true, Steve had that faint half-smile on his face, as if he might just be laughing at *you*, inside. But he looked like that all the time. People didn't like that, either.

" 'Course," said Dunk.

"What's it like?" said Steve. "This ... Flip Flop."

Dunk gave a look to the left and the right, as if someone might overhear them. He lowered his voice. "Not so much a *what*," he said, "as a *who*. As for *like*... That I can't rightly say. I never saw he. But my uncle Joe did, and he said he's got web feet like a gurt frog. Stands to reason. That's what makes the sound."

Dunk paused. Even Mr Fairbairn had gone quiet. "Flip... Flop... Flip... Flop..." Dunk said it so quietly that the main sound was the wet slap of his lips. "Coming over the bog towards you in the middle of the night. Or when the mist comes down."

"How did your uncle Joe see him, then?" said Howard. Steve gave him a sharp look. But Dunk's round glasses looked Howard straight in the eye.

" 'Cause he had a flashlight, stupid."

"Was ... was he all right?" said Howard. "He wasn't killed or anything?"

"Not he," Dunk grinned. "Mind you, he was always a bit peculiar after it, was Uncle Joe."

" 'Damn!" Steve had slipped to the corner of the hut and

peeped round. "Shift!" he hissed, ignoring Dunk. "They've gone. We'll miss them." When they got to the changing room there was nothing in there but the smell of socks and cold sweat. In the corner their two bags were propped up together, with a pencilled note: SEE ME TOMORROW, YOU BOYS. GORDON FAIRBAIRN.

As they slunk out of the field by the back gate, Howard noticed that they weren't the last ones there. Up a small rise, Dunk was standing quite still, peering through the wire of the fence. Howard looked where the assistant groundsman must be looking, out beyond the fresh brick of the school, beyond the gardens of the new Belleview Estate. Last year there had been cows on that hillside. Now, bright orange-brown fences carved up squares of bare earth. Dads like Steve's were plotting patios. Grass and weeds were just coming out of shock and starting to regrow. But lift your eyes a bit, above it all, and there was the view.

Three dark hills rose in silhouette against the sky, close-shouldered as a rugby scrum. That was Dartmoor, just the start of it. On the top of the middle hill were two tors, piles of rock that must be as big as houses really, but from five miles off they looked like pillars of a gate. And beyond, out of sight, was the heart of the moor. It seemed to Howard that Dunk, too, was miles away. For all his mole's sight and his pebble glasses he seemed to be staring at the things you couldn't see, out there, beyond that open gate.

2.

"Howard? Is that you?"

The hallway in the narrow terraced house was dark, though it was only half past six. He reached for the switch. It still didn't seem bright, not 100-watt bright, the way other people's houses were. He thought: we're just 40-watt people, Mum and me. There was a flicker beneath the lounge door.

"Howard?" Her voice had a sharp edge this time, as if she really thought it might be a burglar or an axeman.

"Yes, Mum."

She was perched on the edge of the sofa, as he knew she would be, waiting. On the TV screen, a presenter in a grey suit closed in with a bad-news voice. It was an in-depth exposé of the kind Howard knew his mum especially disliked. One night she had stayed up watching a whole hour about childhood leukaemia, worrying herself sick, just to punish him.

"Well?"

She laid aside a pile of mending. She always had it by her, Howard's mum. He never seemed to see or wear the mended things again, but he couldn't imagine her without her needle – stab, stab – getting quicker when she was anxious or angry. There was always mending to be done.

"You're late."

"Sorry, Mum. Missed the bus." Howard took a step back into the hall. "I stopped at Steve's house."

"Don't just drop your coat there." As he turned from the pegs she was right behind him, level with his shoulder, looking up. She had been shorter than him for two years now, but still he flinched.

"What's wrong, Mum?"

"You could have warned me. You could have rung. You know what a phone box looks like. Why don't you ever *think*?" She paused a moment. In the dim light of the hall her skin was pale as clenched knuckles. She looked tired. "You know I can't settle if I don't know where you are."

"Can I make you something, Mum? A coffee?"

"Coffee? After six o'clock? I don't sleep well at the best of times, you know that. Coffee, I ask you!"

"Mum, Mum, I said I'm sorry. Can we have supper?"

"Supper's spoiled, of course..." He could see from the cabbage that reached the table that she had cooked for six o'clock precisely. It must have been warming in the oven ever since, going crisp at the edges like burnt greaseproof paper. She had probably turned the gas up, just to rub it in.

"Now..." She sat opposite him, with a portion half the size of his own. "Aren't you going to tell me anything about school?"

"It was only sports practice. It's Sports Day tomorrow."

"Sports Day? I must get your kit washed."

"Don't worry. I'm not in anything." Just for a moment, he thought, she looked genuinely surprised. *Mum...* How could he say it? *I mean ... LOOK at me!* But it was no good. She just couldn't see.

It wasn't that Howard was fat. There was just a bit too much of him in all directions. Howard bumped into things – and into people, too, so they'd turn and he'd have to apologize, fast. His long legs didn't work for running; his size just made him a soft target. Easy prey. Team games were no better. Howard was the kind of kid that when you did pair work in class, he'd always be the one without a partner, even when you *knew* there was an even number in the room.

The instant whip, whipped hours earlier, had a kind of dusty crust on it. Howard ate it as quickly as he could, without looking too closely.

"This Stephen, you never tell me anything about him. Or his family. Are his parents nice?"

Howard shrugged. "Steve's just a friend. His mum and dad are . . . just a mum and dad. Ordinary, I suppose."

"What's that supposed to mean?"

Howard closed his eyes. There was a kind of swarming feeling in his head, and his chest felt tight, the way it did when he couldn't get out of games at school.

"Can I go upstairs, Mum?"

"What's wrong? Are you ill?"

"I'm just tired. Can I go now?" He heaved to his feet.

"Howard, come back. Don't just walk away when I'm talking to you. Howard!"

From half-way up the stairs he looked back. Mum was gripping the banisters, looking through at him as if one or the other of them was in a cage. He opened his mouth, but there was nothing he could say. He shook his head.

"That's right, go on, go away by yourself. It's all very well. Don't you ever think what I go through? All these years, all I've ever wanted . . ." Her voice quivered. "All I've ever wanted is the best for you. I've done my best, God knows. And now you've started staying out late, like all the others." She was following him upstairs; she stopped, head level with his feet. "You're the only one I've got. You know what I always say: I've put all my eggs in one basket. Can you imagine . . .?"

Howard shut the bedroom door very carefully. He was trying to imagine anything but a basket of eggs. He sat down on his creaky bed carefully, as if the slightest sound might start an avalanche.

What would Steve do? Steve said things like, "The old man was in one of his moods last night. Did a bit of shouting, you know, the way dads do . . ." Then he'd stop. "Sorry." If there was one thing everybody knew about Howard, it was that he didn't have a dad. Nothing particularly strange about that, but it had stayed that way for years. When Mum turned up for parents' things at school, she was always alone. From the look of her face, that tight look round the mouth, with lines like an old lady's already, she would stay that way.

Basket of eggs. Howard leaned his back against the bedroom door and tried to breathe. A weight was pressing in around his ribcage – dark little room, dark little house, dark little family . . . It was all too tight. *Basket of eggs.* Something was going to crack.

Some time later, Howard heard her moving around downstairs, putting clothes on to clothes horses, taking them off. On a bad night she might keep it up past midnight, then come down to breakfast in the morning looking like a ghost. When he was sure she wasn't coming up, he went to the old toy cupboard and took out his secret place. It was only an old box from a game of Picture Lotto, hidden behind a massacre of Action Men with lost arms and legs at impossible broken angles. He opened the box and slipped out the booklet inside.

DISCOVER SOUTH-WEST DARTMOOR: 20 Day Trips For The Whole Family had been dog-eared for years. Howard did not quite know why he kept it, but somehow it seemed right because it was where he found the photograph. It was slipped in at page 19, marking some excursion they would not go on now, because Mum did not drive. You could see why the photograph got used as a bookmark. The only wonder was why it hadn't gone straight in the bin. Howard handled it carefully, as if it might smudge.

The light was in the wrong place, glaring from behind a figure who was only a silhouette, with arms out resting on two gate posts and head at an angle that might have said something if Howard could have seen the face. As it was, he could not even tell if the figure was looking at the camera or away.

Downstairs in the bookcase was the family album. There wasn't much in it except Howard, or sometimes Howard and his mum when she'd asked somebody else to snap them at the beach. His image, half his age now, smiling goofily because he had been told to, made Howard feel sad. But sometimes he leafed through the album for the things that weren't there.

He could see sets of rips in the paper where photo corners had been. Near the start there were several sets on each page, gone. Only once had he asked about the missing photos. "Oh," said Mum. "They were no good." She said it quickly, but there was something in her voice that made him never ask again. The spaces stopped suddenly alongside pictures of Howard aged, maybe, four.

Howard stared at the silhouetted figure, letting his eyes unfocus as if it was one of those puzzles that could be a vase or two faces. He could not imagine what he might see, if only his mind could make the click. He could not even work out where the place in the photo was. If that was a gate there should have been something beyond it – a street, a garden or a house. But the light was so bad there was nothing, just a white blur. The figure could have been stepping out of, or gazing out into, fog.

Even then, years ago, when Howard has knocked *DIS-COVER SOUTH-WEST DARTMOOR* off the shelf by accident, and the bookmark slid out, he had known at once he must not let Mum see. He must fight back the wish to ask her: *That's Dad, isn't it?* He would lose either way. The answer might be No ... or it might be Yes, and the photo would go where the others went years ago – in the bin.

He slipped it back in at page 19, put the booklet in the box and the box in the cupboard. As he quietly, firmly, closed the door he thought of the other doors – his room, the porch, the front door – closed like airlocks in a space ship lost in orbit, with the oxygen dwindling slowly, it getting ever harder to breathe. He shut his eyes and tried to beam himself some-where, anywhere, as long as it was far away.

What's the farthest away thing you can think of? Howard stretched out, thinking. Scenes from books were no good. Then it was there in his mind's eye, clearer even than that afternoon: the edge of the moors, with clouds behind it, clouds and wind.

It would be a big dream, he knew as he came to the edge of it; it would be a steep dream, made of granite. He would have to pace himself, climbing, so he didn't lose his breath. It was slow, but he was getting somewhere. The Gate was in sight. For hours, the gateposts were coming nearer, hours and hours. They were getting bigger; they were huge. From behind came a glow of light, but it was still too far above him; he couldn't see through.

The Wind Gate. As he thought the words, the wind started blowing. It grew stronger, so it pushed him backwards and he had to bend double to push his way on. Then the thing began to close – two huge gates hinging slowly into place. He was straining towards them, gasping. *Wait!* he was trying to shout. Just before the great gates came together, Howard saw the man.

He was only an outline, a small silhouette in the narrowing crack, but with the light behind he cast a long thin shadow, down the hillside right to Howard's feet. Just as the gate closed, clunk, Howard could not be certain: was it the gate-keeper, locking it against him? Or when he raised his arms like that was he waving: *Let me out?*

3.

"Well?" said Steve. "What are you afraid of?"

"It's not that..." Howard looked round furtively. They had ducked in behind the kitchens, half-way to the playing field. "We can't just ... *go*."

"Why not?"

"Well ... Fairbairn, for one thing. He said see him."

"Nah. He won't remember, not on Sports Day – not when he can watch all those others suffering. Let him play with his starting pistol in peace. Be cool."

Steve lounged against an industrial-sized dustbin, ignoring the smell of three days' dinners. He seemed to be the only still thing in the school. Everyone else was hurrying out of Registration, grabbing their lunch packs or kit bags, making for the field. "You've never bunked off before, have you?"

"It's not that..." said Howard again, flushing. He came to a stop.

"Want to cheer your team on, do you? Go for it, Yellows, ra-ra-ra?" Steve gave that look of his, as if he might just yawn. "Suit yourself."

"I don't understand. Why today?"

Steve shrugged. "Because ... I've had it up to here. I've had enough of this place. This time last year I was in *London*." He glanced round once, and the school, Belleview, the whole of Plymouth, became as silly as a seaside model village. "I've had enough of all these cretins – present company excepted... Well, one of us. And it's just as bad at home. If I hear my mother say 'It's such a beautiful view' one more time I'll start smashing things." The way he said it, Howard believed him. "So there isn't a shop on the whole estate? So the bus into town runs every other Thursday when there's an R in the month? So what? We can look at the *beautiful* view!" Steve slung his bag across his shoulder. "I'm off."

Howard hesitated long enough for Steve to reach the corner. A bunch of boys he knew went by, jostling and joshing, sharing private jokes. "Hey," he called after Steve. "Wait for me."

"What do we do now?" he said as he caught up. Steve cut suddenly to the left, down the back of the kitchens where the cooks went, straight through the back yard, quick but casual, and they were in Shackleton Close outside. "Now?" Steve grinned. "We hit the road!"

Howard laughed uneasily. "You've seen the films," said Steve. "Two buddies hijack a car. They're on the run – just done a bank job or something. So they head out west. Small towns, motels, down the Interstate. Then the music starts up . . ." He tapped his Walkman. "*Born To Be Wi-i-ild* . . . And they're in the desert. Great!"

"Did you say hijack?"

"Well, we can get a bus to start with."

"Where are we going?"

"Oh . . ." Steve mimed tossing a coin. "Anywhere. Down town?"

"No!" Howard said suddenly. Steve looked up sharply from the imaginary coin. He'd never heard Howard say No, not really *No*, before. But Howard was not looking at him. His

gaze went out and up, over his shoulder. Steve followed his
eyes, to the edge of the moors.

"That's it," said Howard quietly.

"Hey, do me a favour," Steve said. "Leave that to the
Scouts." No reaction. "Hey, Howie..." Howard did not
move. That *was* peculiar. He didn't like his name. (Who gave
a kid a name like that? He'd never met another Howard,
except dead, in books.) But he always winced when anybody
called him Howie, even Steve.

"You want a desert?" said Howard. "There it is."

Steve looked at him sidelong. He was all right, was Howard,
whatever people said, though he *did* take things too seriously.
This was no joke.

"Fair enough." OK, why not, they had a day to kill. Steve
plugged in his headphones as they slunk, quickly but warily,
down to the bus stop. Skeleton Crue got into action with a
bass line like a boxer coming out for the first round.

KRRRANG!
There's a way
KRRRANG!
You gotta find
KRRRANG!
Outa this world
KRRRANG!
Outa your mind...

Steve's hair flounced with the beat. Shame Howard couldn't
hear it with him. Then again, who knew what went on in
Howard's head? A few days later, lots of people would be

asking that – teachers, parents, nice policewomen. But right now a bus appeared, just on cue, and they were on the road.

"How far on to the moors do you go?" asked Howard.

"Daws Cross," said the driver, with a sour look. "Both ways?"

"Pardon?"

"You coming back?"

Howard nodded hard and, predictably, blushed.

"Well, I don't know, do I?" said the driver, and gave the gears a mean jolt. They were travelling.

"Relax." Steve stretched out on the back seat. Howard sat up straight and tight. "We're on holiday."

"He *looked* at us ..."

"Be cool. You think he's one of your mum's spies? Take it easy." Steve nudged his lunch bag. It clanked. Two Mars bars, several bags of crisps and a couple of cans of lager.

"Where did you get those?"

"Dad can't count. Not once he's started... Daws Cross? You know the place, do you?" Howard didn't look as if he did. Steve didn't mind. "No probs. We've got all day."

The bus was almost empty. Three old biddies with armour-piercing voices were taking it in turns to fear the worst for old Mrs Mullins in the nursing home. "Mind you," said one. "She's always been a bit, you know..."

"Well, you would be, wouldn't you," said another, "after that?"

The bus made an *oooof!* sound and a long groan, as if someone hád just punched it in the stomach. Then with a jolt they were over the rise and Dartmoor opened up enormous arms to greet them. The skyline was too wide to see all at once; it could have been drawn with one sweep of a pencil, without a tree or house or any fiddly detail. It was as smooth as a whale just breaching in a sea of greyish green.

At the roadside was a wooden fence. Between bracken and gorse, shaggy horses ripped the grass. "Look," said Howard.

"A-a-a-aw... My Little Pony!"

The bus pulled up. There wasn't a bus stop in sight, or a house or anything. The man at the roadside didn't say a word as he got on, and neither did the driver. The old man – there was a cindery stubble on his scalp and chin – sat half way back and dumped a small sack of fur on the floor beside him.

"What is it?" Howard nudged Steve. A couple of flies were circling. "Is it dead?" A polythene bag was tied round the limp thing's head with a thick rubber band. They could see dribblings of red inside.

"Rabbit?" Steve guessed. With its legs stretched out, it looked as big as a dog. The man turned round. "Rabbit?" He showed the boys a few grey teeth. "Have some respect for the dead. She's a little moonpuss. Hare, to you." He patted the corpse as if to soothe its feelings. "And what are you two doing this way when you ought to be in school?" He made a wheezy sound that might have been a chuckle. "Don't you worry. Never could be doing with school, meself."

"We're climbing," Howard pointed. "That hill, there. The one with ... the gate."

"Are you, now? Staddle Tors? Used to walk up that way often. Knew a girl up by Morrishtown. Blacklake. Farm's gone now, of course. Lake means a stream, by the way. Town means a couple of houses."

"And bog means a muddy puddle, does it?" Steve was getting fed up with this geezer and his private joke.

"Ah, no, that it doesn't." The old man leaned back so they smelt his breath like pickled onions. "Bog means bog. Watch out for they."

"Or the Hairy Hands'll get you," Steve murmured.

"The Hairy Hands, eh? You know about the Hands? Well..."

"It's true, then?" said Howard.

"I'm not saying I've seen anything, not meself. But there was this convict, see, got out. Hitched a lift, he did, then pulled a knife on the driver and his missus. Left the poor beggars tied to one of them Don't Feed The Ponies signs, just as the mist came down..." He paused.

"Well?" said Steve.

"They..." pronounced the old man slowly, "was the lucky ones... Found the car next morning. It had swerved off, right into the bog. Off a long straight road, mind you, and nothing coming either way. Just swerved off, sudden. He was dead, the convict was, of course. And on his face, all round the eyes, gurt bruises, and five long straight gashes, like from claws."

"Don't you believe him, dearie." One of the women had looked round. "Don't you go giving them ideas, Stanley. Wicked old bugger, he is." The bus jolted and stopped. "Daws Corner," called the driver.

"That's right." The old man grinned with a small hiss like a pressure cooker. "Wicked lies. Morrishtown," he called after them. "That's your best way." A fit of wheezing caught him.

For a second Howard thought: he's dying, not laughing at all. But the old man caught his breath. "And don't you go no further than the Gate."

4.

"So much for the village idiot—" Steve said as the bus pulled away. "Now what?" But Howard wasn't listening.

Daws Cross had a nerve, calling itself a *place*. It was a crossroads with a garage forecourt, shut and boarded up, with petrol pumps standing to attention like suits of armour in a stately home. As for Dartmoor . . . Where were the mountains, Steve thought. Where were the bogs that everyone went on about? What's the big deal? There was the same view of three hills they had seen from the field, just nearer. In between was a valley full of stone walls. It looked like a jigsaw picked up at a jumble sale: all the pieces the same two colours and you can bet there'll be one missing at the end. "Is this it?" said Steve. But Howard wasn't listening.

He was staring out towards the moor. "That's it," he said quietly, as if to himself. Steve came up behind him, scuffing his trainers in the gravel, but Howard did not look round. He stood like they'd seen Dunk standing, motionless, the day before; Dunk, the assistant groundsman, the head-case. "We can do it," Howard said. "We'll have to walk a bit."

"Hang on. This is a road movie. Who said anything about *walking*?"

"That's the place." Howard's gaze was fixed on the two rock-piles of Staddle Tors. As he turned and smiled, slowly, Steve had an uneasy feeling. It was that smile. Usually Howard grinned quickly, eager to please; he bobbed up and down a bit, like a puppy asking for a pat. Now only his lips moved. "That's where we're going," said Howard and it wasn't a suggestion; it was a statement of fact. The Howard Steve knew *never* talked like this.

"Hey, Howie... What's got into you?" Steve heard himself say. He'd seen the films, he'd read the books, where someone got *possessed.* A dybbuk or a voodoo spirit moved in, squatting in their body, speaking with its own weird voice, till an exorcist came and there'd be blood and vomit. Usually, Steve liked that bit.

"Nothing." Howard blushed and gave a little giggle, like the Howard Steve's parents liked ("Such a nice boy. Quiet..."), who said Thank You for his milk and biscuits twice. Still, he turned to the road. "Let's start walking," he said.

OK, thought Steve, have it your way. This place was so boring, they might as well make for somewhere else. And Howard was already on his way.

Steve didn't bust a gut to catch up. He knew Howard: he couldn't keep this pace up. Steve had seen him on enough cross-country runs. The two of them were always last together, but that was because Steve *liked* being last. It was his way of telling old Fairbairn: *I'm not putting myself out for you.* But Howard always really tried. He would puff, he would gasp. He just wasn't built for it.

"Hold on," said Steve, after a while. "This is stupid. It's miles. I'm going to hitch."

Howard swung round. "You can't do that."

"Why not?"

"Well..." Howard's face was pink already, from the fresh air and the walk. "It's not safe." Steve shook his head and stuck his thumb out. "Suit yourself." Almost at once there was a crunch of tyres, and Steve turned to look up . . . and up to where a lorry bulked above them. It was camouflage-splotched: green, khaki, grey.

"You, lad! Yes, you. Where do you think you're off to?" The sergeant's trimmed moustache was thin and sharp. Steve pulled his denim jacket over Skeleton Crue and flicked back the hair from his face but it was too late. The sergeant was used to raw material. Every year lads turned up with their styles and fashions. He made soldiers of them. "Well? Speak up."

"We're making for Morrishtown, sir." Howard turned to stare. Steve had never called anybody *sir* before. "It's a challenge. A kind of initiative test."

The sergeant nodded slowly. "Well, well... Better than hanging round the streets. I like your spirit. Though I'd have your goolies for your get-up, if you were one of my lads. Climb in the back." He jerked a finger at Howard. "Your mate too. Get a move on."

Arms reached down from the back of the lorry and hoicked them up; the lorry jolted and was rumbling on. The floor where Howard had landed was bare metal, and the first thing he could make out in the khaki gloom was boots. The soldiers were ranged along the sides with their kit, and Steve and Howard were in the middle in a heap.

"Whit's tha' ferChrissake? A couple o' frigging natives?"

"Shut it, Cameron." The sergeant craned round from the front. "These lads are with us till Morrishtown. Set 'em a good example. Show 'em what the army's done for you."

"Yes, Sarge." Cameron treated his mates to a private grin,

but sat back. Game over. Gradually Steve noticed something about the men around them: they were just a few years older than himself and Howard, that was all.

"How long've you been in the army?" Steve said. It sounded wrong, he knew, but he had to say something. Howard would have huddled there and blushed all day.

"Five honderd friggin' years," Cameron said. He slumped back, staring out at the road behind them.

"Couple of months, maan. First manoeuvres." It was a bright voice. And a black face – the only one there.

"You don't have to sound so friggin' pleased about it, Jimbo." This came from back in the gloom, half-mumbled. "Ain't no jungles on the moor for you to swing in."

"Watch it, maan."

"OK, OK..." This voice was Welsh; it tweaked up at the end of each sentence, as if everything was a question. "Cool it. Going into the moor, you two? Or just a nice little stroll?"

"Staddle Tors," said Howard.

"My, there's heroic..." The Welsh lad's long, thin face was deadpan.

"You be careful, maan. It's a serious place. You need equipment. What you got on your feet?"

Steve stuck out his feet. His trainers were a better brand than Howard's, but suddenly that didn't seem to count for much. "Hot stuff," said the Welsh one, drily.

"It's no joke, maan. People die out there."

"You be careful now, serious." The Welshman wasn't teasing now; he sounded like an uncle, which was worse.

The lorry hit a humpback bridge. Half of them piled on to the floor. There was a lot of swearing as they scrambled back upright, and Steve and Howard were forgotten. The mumbler made another crack about monkeys and jungles, and the black lad got one back about Millwall, and the others nudged and grinned. Then the sergeant cracked the whip – a quick "Shut it". And they did.

Howard looked around. Steve was doing his best to look casual, but it wasn't easy. He was in the wrong film now. They didn't meet each other's eyes. These were the big boys – all in the team together, even the ones who were just about to come to blows. A few of the others were talking now and then in twos and threes, and the few words Howard caught meant nothing to him at all. They talked in initials and nicknames, like another language. Howard and Steve were no one, nowhere. They weren't even tourists. No one gave them a phrase book for the land where soldiers talk like that.

Then Howard saw it again, in his mind's eye. When he thought of that skyline, with the Wind Gate open and all the wildness of the moor beyond it, everything else went very small and clear. When he had followed Dunk's gaze yesterday he had known, somewhere inside, that this was not the first time he had seen the Gate. And at Daws Cross, there'd been a jolt inside him like a small electric shock. The moment he tried to lay hold of it, it was gone. All he had left was a smell like sadness, dusty and rubbery, and a glimpse of his own fingers picking at a loose seam, leaking its stuffing, in the back seat of a car. But his mother hadn't got a car...

There was a lurch, and more cursing and jostling. "Morrishtown," the sergeant called back. "Shift." As Howard tried to stand, his knees went all jellied. He slithered back out of the lorry as clumsily as he had tumbled in. He hoped no one would be looking back to see him staggering to his feet, but of course Cameron was. He was still staring out exactly as he had since he last spoke, with the same sneer on his hard-edged, acne-spattered face. But he wasn't looking at Howard or Steve or anything that was here. His mind was on something else, hundreds of miles away. He might have been thinking of home.

5.

Steve knew what Dartmoor was meant to be like. He'd seen *The Hound of the Baskervilles* on late-night TV. It was black-and-white, or seemed that way; people staggered about in a dry-ice mist between papier mâché Stonehenges that wobbled in the fight scenes. But no one had told him the main thing about Dartmoor. It was a mess.

Everything Steve could see was a leftover: that railway carriage at the bottom of the field, with a few hens scratching round it. That dead tractor in the bracken, with moss growing round the hubs where tyres used to be. The place wasn't there to be looked at. *Town kids!* it seemed to say. *You can think what you like.*

The track gave up on them. It had only been leading to one last house, hidden by a thorn hedge and a barbed-wire gate. Everything about it said KEEP OUT. As they looked, the dogs exploded, scuffling and snarling. Steve snarled back. The creatures went into a frenzy, battering the gate. He grinned. "Why are dogs so stupid?"

The barking faded behind them as they climbed. It wasn't easy. Howard took a breather, leaning on a rock. From here, the last house looked like what it was – an outpost. He could see why the dogs barked. By night, there'd be wild things – foxes, maybe worse. There'd been a story in the papers years ago: a convict broke into a farm and held a woman hostage with a carving knife. Howard's mum had immediately put the paper away and several days later little Howard found it in the bin.

"Yes," Howard murmured. "This is where it starts." They'd been walking happily enough, side by side. Every now and then Steve would do his Mr Fairbairn imitation – "*Go on. Push yourselves. Make it hurt!*" – and they would laugh. The thought of all the others on the school field, sweating and cheering, was as good as a rest. Now, suddenly, Howard was still, as if sniffing the air like a wild thing on a scent.

"Where what starts?" said Steve.

"The moor. The real moor. Can't you feel it?"

Steve looked around. "It's OK," he said. "For an afternoon stroll. I don't know what everyone makes such a fuss about."

"You heard what the squaddies said: It's serious." Howard had that wide-eyed innocent look that Steve knew well. You could spin him any yarn and he'd believe you. Steve used to, at first, till he realized it was just too easy. Besides, Howard was all right. He was a friend.

"Nah," Steve said. "That's another fairy story, like your Flip Flop and your Hairy Hands. Spook city!" Howard did not like Steve when he sneered. He turned away. "You don't *believe* that stuff?" said Steve.

"Of course not. Not really. But . . ." Howard did not turn round. "But you can understand it, can't you? When you're actually here, I mean. Even if it is only stories. A place like this must sort of . . . soak them up." He was just hoping Steve wasn't going to ask him what he meant, because he wasn't sure, when something tapped him on the shoulder. Howard looked, and squealed, and flinched away.

"It's only a skull," said Steve.

"Yugh. Put it down."

"It's clean. I found it in the stream."

"That's a dead sheep. There'll be germs."

Steve knew that voice of Howard's. Just like his mum. Far from putting it down, Steve balanced the skull on his head like a hat. His Skeleton Crue T-shirt gave a sidelong smirk. "Silence, mortal..." Steve did his hundred-year-old-man voice. "Silence for the Ritual of the Horned God!"

"Stop it! STOP IT!" Before Steve could take it in – this was Howard, *shouting* at him – the skull had been swiped off his head, landing with a rustle in the bracken. "Hey, cool it," said Steve. "Only a joke." When Howard did not reply he said sullenly: "We've been walking for *hours*. When's something going to *happen?*"

There wasn't a path any more. There were dips and slips between the stones where you could turn an ankle, just like that. "Sorry," said Steve, after a while. Then all at once they were there. They came on to the rise and the moor opened up beyond them, miles wide and high as the sky. What they had climbed was a foothill. Ahead was a slope like a painter's palette splashed with purple, yellow, green and grey. There were long spreading slides of boulders, as if a tor had been stepped on and smeared like a snail. Howard leaned on a rock and felt that electric-shock thrill again. He was touching Dartmoor – like touching a piece of dangerous machinery, in a saw-mill maybe, when you're almost sure it's not turned on.

"Look!" said Steve. "An eagle." At last, this was the right kind of movie. He could almost hear *Born To Be Wild*. High up over their heads, a buzzard with spread wing-fingers and a flared tail circled slowly, then slid out across the valley, over scattered villages and the crossroads where Daws Cross must be, taking their gaze out to the crinkle of skyline that was Plymouth, and beyond that the wide grey sea.

Howard glanced at his watch. If they were at Sports Day now it would be lunch-time. So lunch-time it was. "What would your dad say?" he said between bites. "If he knew we were here?"

"He'd go mad a bit, that's all."

"What does he do? Does he ... hit you?"

"Hardly ever. Does your mum?"

"That's different..." Howard frowned. "Isn't it?" For a while neither of them spoke. Then Howard said, "We'd better go."

"What's the hurry?" Steve pointed vaguely. "There's your Gate. We're almost there." It was true: there was just a gentle dip, quite bright green at the bottom, between them and the last long slope that led to the top of the moor. On the next hill over, a tall television mast touched the clouds; they were blowing fast, and seemed to snag and tatter where they caught.

"OK, OK." Steve slung an empty can behind the boulder and got to his feet. There was a rumbling sound, deep, from nowhere in particular, like when his dad banged on the ceiling: *Turn that racket down up there.* He frowned, then shrugged his shoulders. "Keep going at this rate, we'll be home in time for tea."

Steve's mum hadn't been back in the house a minute – time to dump the shopping, throw the cold stuff in the freezer, flick on the radio, kick off her shoes and put her feet up – when the phone rang. It was always the way.

"Hello? Sorry? Wait a mo…" The radio was burbling midday news. She clicked it off. "Oh, *Howard*'s mum! I'm Susan. You know what these boys are like. Never occurs to them we've got names of our own…" At the other end, *Mrs Harris* stayed Mrs, no first name. The voice was small and tight.

"No, no," said Steve's mum. "Howard was lovely yesterday. Proper little gentleman. Not like our Stevie! How do you do it?" There was an awkward pause.

"He got home OK, did he? I know he left a bit late, but they seemed to be getting on and, well … you don't like to interfere, do you?" The silence down the line got louder. "Was … was there something? School rang? Oh, old Fairbairn. Trust him. He's always checking up. He's got it in for Stevie. What? Skived off again? His dad'll murder him when he finds out. But look, don't worry. They'll have gone into town, you know the way they do … I expect he'll roll up in a minute…"

In the narrow hallway, Howard's mother put the receiver down. One hand flicked a bit of fluff from the table out of habit, but she was staring at the carpet. It was tired too. All the years of shampooing and hoovering had left it dull. As she stared, her eyes went out of focus and the pattern started to swim, like water underneath you on a narrow bridge, so that she came over all peculiar and had to sit down at the bottom of the stairs.

He had run away. Her Howard. Truanting.

It all added up, slowly, like forensic evidence. He had lied to her. He had got in with a bad crowd. *They'll have gone into town*, that Stephen's mother had said, cool as that. Some parents just don't care. She'd seen the young louts in the precinct. Hanging round. Smoking, most of them, with girls who were almost as bad as they were. Probably shoplifting too. He was going to the bad, her Howard. Her little boy.

She had always known it would happen, but not yet, please not yet. In the nights after Clive left she had tiptoed into four-year-old Howard's bedroom and watched him sleeping with his face all baby-soft. Sometimes she watched so hard it woke him and he stirred. She had thought then: one day he'll be standing there, taller than me, with a deep voice like his father's, lying to me, like they do. One day he'll be gone. Run away, like Clive. Like they do. But please, not yet.

The policewoman who answered the phone didn't seem to take it in. *"I'm sorry, madam, but it isn't two o'clock yet. He's hardly a missing person yet. You'll see, he'll be back after school. Just you calm down and wait a bit. If he isn't back by midnight..."*

Clunk. The receiver went down. Silly woman – Howard's mum could tell she wasn't a mother, that one. Or if she was, *her* children would be hanging round the precinct, getting into trouble with the law.

She bundled her coat around her. The school should be doing something. She would see to it they did. And if they didn't, she'd just have to start the search herself.

6.

High above Howard and Steve the larks were shrilling: *easy! easy!* It was downhill now on grassy paths, in and out of clumps of gorse. Steve raced ahead. Dartmoor might not be Nevada, but it was OK. Round a bush he ran into a herd of cattle. The horns were as wide as the path and hooked up meanly at the ends. There was a split second's stand-off, then the front one crashed away through the bracken. The others shambled after it like wardrobes on the move. "Hey, see that?" said Steve. "Those horns! I'd like one of *those* skulls..."

The next bit looked easy, and green as a lawn. Up on the rise to their left a file of hikers in bright cagoules, heading back the way Steve and Howard had come, seemed to stop and stare at them. The leader waved. Steve waved back, briefly. "Hey, Howie... Race you," he called and leaped a stream that had seeped out of nowhere. Splut: his foot sank and he staggered. Thick black mud sagged back in to fill the foothole, with a little gulping sound. One trainer filled up completely, and it smelled like his dad's compost heap. He balanced upright and waved to Howard. "No probs," he called. "Bit wet, that's all. Follow me."

Half an hour later Howard was clinging to a tussock on his hands and knees. "Steve, wait." All around them there were troughs of bare peat, black, like uncooked Christmas pudding. "What's that noise?"

There was a faint wet slap behind them. "Over there..."

No . . . There!" A pock mark quivered in the ooze. Another, close up, broke with a sound like a horrible kiss. "There's your Flip Flop." Steve was laughing. "Marsh gas. He's coming to get you!" he crowed. "OK, OK . . . If you're worried . . ." He turned round. "Yugh . . ."

A step or two behind him was an open bag of meat. The sheep was half sunk, two legs poking upwards, stiff and straight. It seemed to have been unzipped from its throat to its tail; there was a black cave where the innards might have been. A bit of a tube or a bulgy gobbet still hung at the edge as if it had flowed out molten then set, like lava, and the head craned back towards them, gazing from sockets which glistened not with eyes, but flies.

Back on firm ground, twenty minutes later, they took their socks off to dry. Their feet were cold straight away; the flesh was swollen pale and wrinkly, like Howard had once read drowned bodies are. "Sod this," said Steve. "Let's go back."

"No! The Gate . . ."

"We near enough got there. Who'll know?"

"*I'll* know. Steve, please . . . Just up this hill . . ." They both looked up. There was no sign of the Gate. The three big hills had somehow vanished. The moor had looked so open and welcoming half an hour ago; now it had closed around them. They were on the inside and could not see out.

"There's the TV mast." Only the stump of it showed, like a stick poked in a stream of cloud. The whole sky had a muddy look.

"Where?" said Steve. By the time Howard pointed, the mast had gone. He thought he saw a faint trace of it in the greyness, but the clouds were blowing and swirling so he couldn't focus. He looked at another hill and thought he glimpsed it there too. And the next.

"I'm fed up," said Steve. "Don't know about you, but I'm going home."

"You can't!" Howard was very still. People never thought of him as big. He always seemed smaller than his body, somehow. Now, for the first time, Steve noticed how tall Howard really was. "You can't just go back," he said.

"Oh, yeah? Who's going to stop me?"

Howard knew that look. The coiled spring. Once, someone called Steve "shortarse" in the playground and there was a moment, just a moment, when things went so still you could have heard the kettle boiling in the staffroom, two floors up. "Of course I can't *stop* you," Howard said. He bit his lip. "I didn't make you come."

Steve relaxed. "That's all right then, isn't it?" He turned on his heel. "Let's get going."

Ten paces on, Steve turned. "Well?" he said. "Come on." Howard did not move. He looked as though he'd taken root.

"You can't stay there all day," said Steve. "I'm going. See you."

Ten more paces. "Don't be stupid," Steve called. "Come on." Howard shook his head.

"Look, fathead," said Steve, through clenched teeth. He had retraced his twenty paces. Howard made him do it, and Steve didn't like that. He glared, waiting for Howard to shrivel, but he didn't, though he blinked a bit. "I mean, I can't just leave you here."

"Why not?"

"Because! Because... what would your mum say if I left

her darling Howie out here on the moors?" That should have
got him. But it didn't. "And what would my dad do?" Steve
added.

Howard shrugged. "Sorry." He turned to go. "See you."

"I can't believe this," Steve called after him. "You'll get
lost. You'll have one of your out-of-breath things. You'll pass
out in a bog. You'll ... you'll go and die or something.
Remember what the squaddies said: It's serious out there."
Howard was almost out of earshot. Steve caught up with him.
"Where do you think you're going anyway?"

Howard did not have a chance to answer. Instead, they both
looked up. There was that rumbling again. It felt like someone
thumping on the inside of the moor.

Howard had been on a school trip once to the Theatre
Royal. He couldn't remember the play, but he'd never forgotten the moment when the stage went dark and little men in
black ran on and started shifting scenery about. You were
meant to pretend they weren't there, but he was riveted. Since
then, he'd often dreamed of stage hands running out when
they thought no one was looking, rearranging bits of the
world. The sound the stage sets made, dragged in the dark,
was just the sound he heard now.

In the sky there was no sign of thunder. In fact, it was
clearing. Lark song started up again. As Howard looked up, a
patch of brightness opened in the mist. Steve followed his
gaze up the hillside. The low cloud was breaking and the Gate
had reappeared.

"I suppose it's not that far really," Steve said. "I can't let
you go by yourself." Howard was already walking. With each
thud of his trainers the turf shuddered, as if it was hollow

down below. When the rumbling came again it seemed to keep pace for a moment, then falter, then keep pace again, as if there was a huge heart down there being massaged back to life. He thought: *the heart of the moor.*

7.

They stumbled on the road before they saw it. They had not seen much for a while. They had noticed the grey clouds over in the west, but here on the moor it was still bright. Next moment a dank mist rose up the hillside at them and everything went grey again. "It's OK," said Howard, none too surely. "It'll pass." Good thing they *knew* the summit was so close.

A car drummed by. They heard it first, not in one place but all around them. The glow of its lights lit the mist. Then suddenly the car materialized, whacked past, and just as suddenly was gone. Not a sound, not a glimmer. That was the weird thing about mist: your eyes and your ears didn't agree any more. Howard heard sheep bleating right behind him, only when he turned there were no sheep in sight. They could be miles away. The more he listened, the more he noticed how sheep sound like people imitating sheep, and not very well, at that.

There was water somewhere – a soft lapping like a large dog drinking. In the banked-up hardcore of the road, a trickle from a broken pipe was cutting itself a gulch. Steve looked up the road.

"You're not going to start hitching again," said Howard.

"Last chance," said Steve. "We could be in a café in twenty minutes. Warm... Dry..."

"We can't give up now."

Steve grinned. "Nah. If we're going to be nuts we might as

well do it properly." Still, neither of them made the first move. There was something about the feel of tarmac. It was a regular road with a dotted white line and it would have a number, B-something-or-other. It would be on maps. It was the last mark of civilization, a frontier. Beyond it, they were really on their own.

There was a shudder of gears; four headlights made a murky halo in the mist. For a moment Steve imagined the sergeant's voice: *You lad, climb in . . .* He couldn't imagine saying No. But it wasn't the army lorry. GREAT ESCAPE EUROCRUISER, said the paintwork, TEWKESBURY. Ten feet up inside his windscreen-wall of glass, the coach driver stared out like the captain of a ghost-ship. Fifty grey-haired faces pressed against the windows down the sides.

The coach had slowed almost to a standstill. Was it going to offer them a lift? Would fifty grannies crowd around them clucking *Poor dear, you'll catch cold*? Over my dead body, Steve thought.

But it wasn't stopping. The faces stared on blankly. Howard and Steve might as well have been sheep or boulders. Just as it passed, Steve jumped up – "Yaaaah!" – and planted two hand-prints on the dripping window. The old dear inside jumped. Then the coach was gone.

"You shouldn't have done that," said Howard. "She might have a heart attack."

"Yaaa-hah!" Steve was prancing around in the road. "Another victim of the Hairy Hands!" He danced down the white line; mist rose to swallow him. His cackling laugh hung in the air. "Steve?" said Howard, after a minute.

"Steve?" said Howard in the silence.

A car came past, an old-fashioned beetle. It came with no sound at all. It was an outline of no colour in the mist. There must have been a family inside but Howard only saw a small boy craning round to gaze out of the back, forlornly, as if there was something he had left behind.

"Steve?" said Howard.

Thud. Hands clamped Howard's eyes. Then Steve was staggering about with laughter. "Got you there! You always fall for that one . . . Howie? You all right?"

I won't . . . thought Howard. *I WON'T get my breathlessness.* The feeling in his chest was of hands clamped round his ribcage from behind, clamped tighter than Steve's hands across his eyes. He sagged forwards, his hands on his knees. The mist sparkled with little stars around him. *Breathe. Relax. Just breathe . . .*

Steve was beside him. "Sorry. Sorry, that was mean. Are you OK?" After a minute Howard straightened up and nodded, but he didn't speak. He was OK. He hadn't given in to it. He'd won.

Howard stepped off the road and led on. Only slightly rising shadows showed which way was uphill, but he knew. Steve followed. If there was one thing *everybody* knew about Steve – teachers, parents, classmates, everyone – it was that he *never* followed. Tell him what to do, he wouldn't do it. But Steve was following Howard now.

The hill was steeper. There still seemed to be a path of kinds, but then it would swerve aside and turn into a sheeptrack, or it would pretend to be a river for a while. There were jumbles of rocks you couldn't skirt and had to scramble. Both boys had to stop for breath.

"It's getting dark," Steve said.

"Can't be. It's only three o'clock." But dark it was, as if they had stepped into the shadow of a mountain. Then the rain began.

At first there were only droplets, settling on their clothes and hair. Then all at once there were great hard splats of water, cold as hail and almost horizontal, driving straight at them. Rain stung their faces and went for their eyes. Before Steve could even think of a swearword foul enough, they were sodden. Around their knees, inside their boots, creeping up to their armpits. It was hopeless.

As Steve came alongside him, Howard was gazing uphill, wincing. Water glistened down his red-raw cheeks, so no one would have known if some of it was tears. "Let's get back to the road," said Steve.

"No. No. It'll pass. We're nearly there." The rain leaned in harder, as if it had heard.

"Are you crazy? You are. You've really cracked. It's this bloody gate thing." Steve grabbed him by the shoulders. "Snap out of it."

Howard was hardly listening. This was like his dream. The Gate was so near, he could almost touch it. Quite what he would find when he got there, he couldn't have said. He didn't need to. He just knew that he would be free. But slowly, with a grinding feeling in his bones, the Gate was closing. Everything – the wind, the rain, the lie of the land and now Steve too – everything was out to stop him getting there in time. He screwed his eyes tight and felt cold watercourses starting through his hair. He had never felt so alone.

"Hey," said Steve. "What's that?" The wind had dropped a little, though the rain was settling to a steady gush. "That sound."

It was a wheeze, then a shivering gasp. Either it was chuckling madly, in fits at its own joke, or else it needed a doctor, fast. The old man on the bus... As Howard opened his mouth to say "It's him..." the sheep came tottering towards them through the mist.

Sheep go around in flocks, everybody knows that. Not this one. They could see at once why no flock would want anything to do with it. Its fleece was peeling off in tatters, leaving almost naked patches like some sort of mange. Its slack-strung belly shuddered with each breath. Its thin, bowed neck hung almost to the ground.

Did it even see them? Howard could have sworn it did, and paused a moment, looking up at them, then barged on by, on a track of its own, zigzagging through the bracken and rocks. "Follow it," he said, as it vanished with a scuffling and a little slip of stones. When the boys reached the place they found the sheep still upright, ambling on into the mist, a few yards down on a flat and grassy track.

STRICTLY NO ADMITTANCE, said the rust-pocked notice. MORRISHTOWN QUARRYING COMPANY... BLASTING... Steve had swanned straight past. "Hold it," said Howard. "That noise we heard earlier – do you think...?"

"No chance," said Steve. "This is ages old." He leaned his trainer on the signpost and gave it a shove. With a mushy tearing sound, the mildewed wood gave way. The sign lay on its back in the rubble, saying NO ADMITTANCE to the sky. The boys followed the sheep.

The track led down, out of the wind. On either side, huge blocks of stone made spiky shadows in the mist – straight-edged chunks, big as doors, with rows of thumb-thick bore-holes on their broken edge. "If it was a quarry," said Howard, "there'll be shelter."

They followed the sheep's disgusting rump, black with mud and caked dribbles of dung. There were wires overhead, that slapped and moaned in the wind, slung from poles that leaned at crazy angles. A drain pipe thick as a leg had cracked away from its wooden supports and swayed to and fro, like a living gargoyle, gushing water in splatters and gulps. Once a diplodocus head – the winch of a rusty conveyer belt – thrust out of the mist above them. Then the square shape hardened in the grey.

It was a wall – the end wall of a house. Roof slates lay broken at their feet. The windows were blind gaps and through the empty door frame they could see a clump of huddling, steaming sheep.

"Great," said Steve. "This was really worth a detour." Then they both looked at each other: was that – yes – the smell of smoke?

8.

"Look, here it is. And again. And again!" Howard's mother stabbed at the pages of the dog-eared exercise book one by one. It lay open on Mrs Blundell's table, next to the chrome-edged stand-up photo of the head-teacher's husband and three grown-up children.

"His rough book," said Mrs Blundell. "They all do the same at his age. We tell them not to, but they can't help doodling."

"Not Howard," said his mother. "That picture... It's the same thing again and again. I found it this morning after breakfast. What does it mean?"

Sports Day... This was all the head needed – a hyperactive parent in panic mode. She had brought her into the office, got a mug of sweet tea in her hands and begun the counselling routine. "I suppose I shouldn't say this," Mrs Blundell confided. "But it's not uncommon for students to go missing on Sports Day, particularly if they're not the sporty type."

There was a quick knock and the Games teacher entered in his sports kit. "I've made enquiries, headmistress," he said. "I hope you realize several events have had to be delayed." He glanced at Howard's mother. "Rest assured that I will have a stern word with the young men in question when they return."

"But where are they? Anything could have happened. And this other boy, Stephen... What do you know about him?"

"Ah, young Stephen," said Mr Fairbairn. "He and I have had words before. His attitude is wrong. Quite wrong."

"I expect," said Mrs Blundell wearily, "they've gone into town. Boys usually do. I suppose I could drive down to the Parade and read the Riot Act—"

"Actually," Mr Fairbairn broke in. "No. The assistant groundsman saw them getting on a bus. In the other direction."

"Not the bus to the moors?" Howard's mother was trembling, so when she held out the rough book it shook. It was true, the same doodle appeared again and again: a three-humped line, and on the middle bump two pillars. It started as a faint outline, like a diagram, but gradually the pencil work got bolder. There was shading in. The hills got darker; clouds massed up behind them, till the only place not smudgy with 2B graphite was the sky behind the Gate. In later sketches two distorted not-quite-human creatures lurked in the shadowy foreground. Beneath one was pencilled: Flip Flop... And the other: Hairy Hands...

"He gets ideas in his head..." Mrs Harris quivered. "He's a good boy, Howard, but ... but he takes things to heart. I know what's happened – this Stephen's started him off. You shouldn't let it happen."

On the hard chair opposite, the head-teacher saw a woman looking old and small. "They'll be all right," she said. The Games master was shifting from foot to foot. He had to get on. In a minute one of these women would start crying, and that would never do. "Thank you, Mr Fairbairn. Better get on with the sports."

All of a sudden Howard's mum was fumbling for a tissue

and her tea was slopping as she put it down. "Look what I've done. I'm so sorry." She stared down at the carpet. "It's different for you. You've got other children, haven't you? Not just the one. And a husband . . ." She dabbed her eyes fiercely. "I'm sorry, but it's true. It's different when there's a man."

It's different all right, thought the head-teacher. But let's not go into *that* now. "Come on," she said. "The boys'll be OK. They're tough."

"No. No, that's just it. Howard isn't. He's always been sickly. It's his chest. He has these breathless spells."

"You mean asthma? Is this on his medical record?"

"Oh, we've seen doctors. You don't get any sense out of them. One of them gave *me* the pills, not him. But I know." She leaned very close. "A mother knows these things. If he isn't looked after properly . . . If he doesn't keep warm . . ." Her fingers closed on the head-teacher's arm. "What are we going to do?"

"Steve, watch it, there's somebody there!"

Steve flattened himself against the mossy wall. "Can't be," he said. "It's a ruin."

Howard stood, dripping miserably. Nowhere was out of the rain. He had started shivering as soon as they reached this place; he couldn't stop. Where he leaned against the outhouse wall, a chill was seeping through. "What's this, then?" he said.

The outhouse still had half a roof. They could not see much of the van because a grey tarpaulin was lashed down tight around it. A fallen branch or two was propped in front as if to hide it, like an army truck in camouflage.

"What a load of junk. Must have been here for years. I

don't know, though . . ." Steve kicked a front tyre; it was firm. The sheep looked up, all their black ears angled at the boys.

"Don't do that," said Howard. "They'll hear."

"Who?"

"I don't know, do I?" Howard shivered. "But they've got a fire."

"Can't be. Look at the place!"

The cottages – two or three, it must have been – were as dire from the back as the front. At this end the roof had gone; the upstairs floor had fallen through. At the other, sheets of rusty corrugated iron had been patched in with the slates. Then both the boys shrank. There was a sound – half rattle, half sigh – like a smoker's lungs. At the upstairs window, a white shape stirred.

"What was it?"

"Stay there." Steve edged back to the corner and very carefully peered round. Suddenly he smiled. Up in the narrow window a sheet of polythene swelled, then crumpled and crinkled, in the wind. Steve gave Howard a nudge. "Woo-woo!" he said, and both of them laughed.

There was a sharp clunk, like the cocking of a gun. They spun round. Up the slope a black goat was tethered on a chain. It stood still, bulging udders swaying, beard tuft wobbling slightly as it chewed. Planks, old doors and wire fenced the bare patch from the cottage to the wooden gate that opened up the hill towards the moor.

Howard shuddered. "You cold?" said Steve. Howard shook his head, and a fine spray of water flew out of his hair, like a wet dog's. The pink of his face was going blotchy, with waxy white cheeks between the scarlet of his nose tip and his ears. "Well I am," Steve said. "If that's smoke, I want a bit of the fire."

"But it could be anybody..."

"And we could catch our deaths. Come on."

As they climbed the fence, the goat lumbered towards them with a wheedling bleat. Pulled up short by the chain, it stared again, then scattered a small pile of droppings behind it. "Thanks, same to you," said Steve.

The door looked old and cracked enough to be history, but there was a lock – a Yale, shiny and new. Steve bent down to squint at the low window. "Don't!" said Howard. Steve did. Nothing happened. After a moment, Howard peered in too. All he could see through the dusty pane was a table covered with a little pile of rubble – stones, some big, some small, mostly cracked open. In among them there were tools – rasps and chisels and tap-hammers sharp as little ice-picks. There was dust and bones.

"Damn," said Steve. "It's empty." Still, he knocked. He swore. He knocked again. He thumped at the door.

Cupping his hands round his eyes, Howard could just make out the flicker from an open fire. At the same time a gust of rain slapped his wet clothes flat against him, all down the back of his legs. He groaned. Steve had stopped swearing.

"Steve?" said Howard. Steve was bent close, wiggling something in the crack of the door. "No!" said Howard. "You can't do that."

" 'Course I can. A kid of six could do it." The phone card slipped once – Steve gritted his teeth and jammed it back and wiggled – then the lock went click.

"You can't! It's br-brrrr..." Howard meant to say

"breaking and entering" but his teeth were rattling and his lips would not move. As Steve opened the door, just a crack, a breath of woody smoky air warmed Howard's face, and his objections melted. "Hurry up," he mumbled. "Let me in."

9.

Inside was dark. The door clunked shut behind them and for a minute they could see nothing at all, except the grey square of the window and the smoking embers of the fire. There were black tongs by the grate, big as a blacksmith's, and some scraps of twisted metal glinting in its light. Gradually the ordinary things appeared: one hard-backed wooden chair, a wicker dog basket with a ripped grey blanket. Some of the shadows were not shadows but tattered hangings draped around the walls.

On the table sat a chipped mug saying BIRTHDAY GIRL, and next to it, the skull.

It was only a sheep, Howard knew that almost straight away. It was just like the one Steve had fooled around with earlier, but polished gleaming white. Between the empty eye-sockets, like a Hindu caste-mark in the middle of the fore-head, was a spike of glassy crystal like an extra horn.

Steve came up behind him. "Weird stuff," he said.

"Let's go," said Howard. "I don't think—" He did not finish the sentence. Just outside, something scrabbled and whined. Then the door thumped open and Howard's breath stopped in his throat. In the dazzle of daylight he could not make out what stood there at all.

The dog was in with one bound. A lean low thing, it came panting and snuffling, sharp nose prodding round their knees and legs, and a low growl in its throat. Steve and Howard froze. Just froze.

Crrunk. The owner tossed a sack towards the fireplace, where it landed with the sound of stone. The dog whimpered and drew back, and the boys could only look up at their host.

The wide khaki cape was silvery with raindrops that dribbled on the stone floor round heavy boots. The head and face were almost hidden by a black sou'wester. The fingerless mitt of the right hand grasped a mallet with a stubby, ugly iron head.

"Excuse me," Steve said very quickly. It was his polite voice, but it wavered. "Sorry, but the door was open and . . ." The dog growled, very low. "Please," he said. "We're wet. We're cold." The figure took one stiff step in – not towards them, but aside. The mallet motioned at the doorway, slightly. *Out*, it said.

"Please!" said Steve. "My friend here's poorly. He's going to have one of his turns."

"No, I'm not!" said Howard. The blood tried to rush to his cheeks but it turned into stars that sparkled in the gloom. He took a step towards the door, which was suddenly miles away and getting further as he blundered and Steve reached out but the floor reached out stone arms to catch him and somehow he was down there with his cheek against a flagstone, looking up.

The figure in the cape did not move. The mallet in its right hand quivered slightly, like a warning. Then the other hand reached up and plucked off the sou'wester, and the head gave one shake, flouncing out a spray of fiery hair.

Howard heard a wheezing sound. It must have been his own breath, he guessed, but as big as the wind on the moor side, and as he passed out, he remembered the man on the bus and the sheep that had shown them the quarry track. Dunk, too. All of them, in the right place at the right time, each step of the way, as if the whole thing had been fixed to lead him here.

"Go on, push yourself! Go!" He's been running for years, though it's only the 100 metres. Something's gone wrong with the playing field – it must be Dunk's fault with his roller – because it's more and more uphill all the time.

He's down, on his hands and knees; it's too heavy to lift, this body of his, and he's gasping for breath but still crawling, like a marathon runner who stumbles in sight of the line. The crowd goes wild, with gusts of cheering like the wind. All the class, all the school are there, and they're amazed, they can scarcely believe it. "Look, it's Howard! Howard's going to win!"

"Go on! Push yourself!" Mr Fairbairn is jogging on the spot beside him, working up a sweat. "We never thought you had it in you." The sergeant is down on the ground beside him, in a string vest, grunting between press-ups: "We'll make a man of you yet."

Howard lifts his eyes to the finishing tape.

At the end of the track waits the Wind Gate. Though there are teachers and kids and close-cut grass and chalked lines all around it, through the Gate ... well, through the pillars of the Gate is somewhere else. Howard can't quite see over the hilltop but there's light there, and there's space, and there is all of Dartmoor, rolling on and on. Just a few metres more and he'll be free, in the wilds, alone.

There's a sweet smell – herbs and honey. There's a woman's voice saying: "Poor thing, he's exhausted. Let him rest."

"Go on! You can make it!" That isn't the Games teacher

shouting. Howard cranes up and he sees it's the Gatekeeper, braced with all his muscles trembling in the narrowing crack. "Don't listen to her. It's a trap! Give in now and she'll never let you go..."

Howard squints at the light. He takes a deep breath, and another, though his heart is thudding so loud that he can hardly hear his own voice when he speaks.

"Dad?" says Howard.

"Hey, Howie... Howie..." That's Steve's voice. What's he doing here, on Sports Day? Howard looks, and as he takes his eyes for a second off the Wind Gate, the stone hinges grind. There is a hollow deep-down rumble as the Gate slams shut.

The woman was facing the window, so all Howard saw when he opened his eyes was her back. And her hair. A flame-thrower gush of orange spread out as wide as her shoulders and down to her waist. Around her head, light caught on wisps of stray hair and faint curls of steam.

She turned round. "I've made you some tea. Sit up." Her eyes were all colours – green, grey, brown, the colours of the moor – and they held him unnervingly still.

The tea was nothing he'd met in a tea-bag – pale yellow and sweetened with honey, just like in his dream. "Camomile," she said, in a voice that told him she could lose patience. "It's not poison. Drink it." It had a faint bitter edge, but the warmth and the sweetness ran straight from his stomach into his veins. "Thank you," he said. Then he blushed. He felt the horsehair blanket tickling his bare knees.

"Don't panic," she said. "Your trousers are by the fire. Flimsy synthetic things – useless for walking. Your friend's jeans are even worse. They get wet through, then they cling.

Don't your parents teach you anything?" If he was a rabbit, she'd be a fox, that look of hers. A vixen. "Do your parents know you're here?"

She was coming into focus, down to the cobweb-fine lines round the corners of her eyes. She wasn't young; she wasn't old. There was dark at the roots of her hair where the henna had grown out. Her thin nose was pierced in one nostril; a stud glinted, a five-pointed star, as she spoke.

"I get it," she said. "They don't. Well, you're on your way home."

"Hold on," said Steve. He was huddled almost in the fireplace, in a blanket of his own. "He's sick."

"Nothing wrong with him except cold and exhaustion. Or you, either. Next clear spell, you walk to the road and start hitching. Someone else can take pity on you." She took Howard's empty teacup and swished out of the door.

Steve sidled over in his blanket. "You OK?" he whispered.

Howard nodded vaguely. "Who is she?" he asked.

Steve leaned close. "Name's Cali. Short for Caroline or something. She's a sort of hippy."

"I thought they were into love and peace."

"She's all right," said Steve. "Really. I just don't think she likes men much."

"Oh, yes?" said Howard. "Has she got a gun?" On the edge of the table, by the stones, were small orange tubes with brass ends. "Aren't those cartridge cases?"

"Shotgun. It's OK, they're dead."

Howard did not look reassured. "It's all weird. Look at that —"

Above the fire was a picture, home-made by the look of it,

scratched with thick charcoal that could have come straight from the fire. There was a woman with her face turned sideways, as fierce as a warrior queen. One arm folded firmly round a thin child, whose face was buried in the woman's long grey cloak.

"New Age goddess stuff," said Steve. "She's into all that. Crystals and things. She gets stones from the quarry. Sells things round the festivals, that's why she's got the old van; she's like a Traveller, only she lives here for part of the year."

"How do you know all that?"

"She told me, stupid. While you were having your little nap."

"How long was I out?"

"Just a few minutes. Quick worker, that's me." Steve smirked. He glanced round. Cali had not reappeared. "You know the trick. Sound interested. Ask questions, then they won't ask you. Adults always fall for it." So that's how he managed to come out of Mrs Blundell's office looking so casual every time.

Cali came through the door. She felt the wet clothes in the fireplace. "What did you do, take a swim in a bog? These'll take hours to dry." Outside there was that deep-down rumbling Howard had heard before. Cali's eyes went to the window. "Where did you think you were going, anyway? They're firing."

"Firing?" said Howard. "Who?"

"Who do you think? The Clay Pigeon Club? The army, of course."

"Hey, great," said Steve. "Can you see from here?"

She whipped round. "Oh, yeah, *great*! Little boys at their

war games. Bang bang . . ." She gazed back out of the window. There was an awkward hush. The wind slapped the polythene upstairs with a tearing sound. "Bang, bang. You're dead."

10.

"I suppose they've got to practise somewhere," Steve said cautiously.

"Practise? It isn't a video game, you know. Those aren't sound effects. They're real shells – made of steel and high explosive. Do you know what shrapnel does?" She scooped up a handful of something from the table and lobbed it at them. Howard flinched under his blanket, Steve jumped back as fragments of metal clattered on the stone. "Hey," said Steve. "That hit me!"

"Pick it up," said Cali. "Go on. Hold one. Take a close look." One piece had bounced and lay on Howard's blanket. He could feel its weight against his leg. Hard to guess what it might have been part of. One end curled back in shreds, slightly blackened, like a steel banana skin. Only the torn edge glinted slightly in the firelight.

"Do they show that in your comics?" said Cali, coldly. "And they haven't *got* to do it, either. *A man's gotta do what a man's gotta do . . .?* They do it because they like it. Just like you – they think it's *great!*"

"I'm sorry," said Steve.

"No you're not. You're just sorry you said it out loud. You're sorry I'm angry. Silly woman, you're thinking, she's making a fuss." They looked up at her so dumbly – two little boys without their trousers – that she smiled, without warmth. "I wouldn't worry, you can't help it. Like father like son . . . It comes of being male."

"That ... that's not fair." Howard's lip was quivering. "I mean, how can you say that? You don't know—"

"I know," she said quietly. "Believe me, I know." There was another rumble, low and flat, like a banging at a huge door: *Let me in.* Cali swore. "That's ours, you know that? These moors belong to all of us; it's a National Park. And then they say: no, you can't go there. Not into the heart of the moor. Sorry, lady, we might just blow your head off." The cold smile again. "Do you know what those words mean: *the heart of the moor?*"

Steve clamped his lips shut. This was like one of those scenes teachers make: *well, boy, what have you got to say for yourself?* and anything you say is wrong. But Howard spoke. "Yes, I think I do. That's where we're going..."

"Not today, you're not," said Cali. "You're getting your things on and you're going home."

"I'm not going home," said Howard.

"Yes, we are," said Steve quickly. "It's only a hill."

Howard gave a firm shake of his head. "The Gate," he muttered.

"Well..." said Cali. "What's this? Mallory and Irving?"

"Who?"

"Two climbers, years ago – nearly reached the top of Everest. Or maybe they got there, maybe they were first – no one knows – they were never seen again. And that," she sighed, "is meant to be heroic. Heroes of the Empire, they were. I expect they had wives and children... Is that it? Want to be a hero?" Howard shook his head again. "What, then? *Because it's there...*"

"Tell her about your precious Gate, then," said Steve.

Howard looked at Steve, and at Cali, and at Steve again. "No," he said. In the awkward pause, Steve bent down and started picking up the shrapnel, piling it carefully back on the table. "Hey," he said. "That's strange."

Among the stones was one cracked open like an Easter egg. In the heart of it, a cave of crystals glittered darkly. In the litter of tools and chippings there were coils of copper and silver wire; there was the skull and odd horns and jawbones; there were bones as fine as needles, maybe birds or mice. And there were pieces of jewellery, half or nearly made.

"That's shrapnel?" Steve hooked up a lumpy pendant by its chain. The metal was dull as it turned in the light of the window, with faint rainbows in it like spilled petrol. Howard shuffled over, his blanket hitched round him like a tartan toga, and leaned close. One edge was melted into blobs like candle wax; one was bent and torn. It looked dangerous to wear. In the middle was a violet glint – a spike of crystal.

"Amethyst," said Cali.

"Is that expensive?" said Steve.

"Semi-precious. There's a lot of it round here, if you've got the patience to look." Steve had moved on to the next piece, and the next.

"Hey, gold –"

"That's right," said Cali, and waited to watch Steve's grin widen. "Iron pyrites," she said. "Fool's gold!"

To one side of the granite fireplace, in a small stone alcove set into the wall, Steve found the largest piece of all. In the light of the tiny night-candle that burned behind it, he saw that the metal had letters etched in it. "R . . ." he spelled out. "O . . . W . . ."

"Leave it," said Cali.

"A... N... *Rowan?* Is that someone's name?"

"I said *leave* it," Cali snapped. "Don't you touch that." The grey-green of her eyes had gone as hard as stone.

"Only looking..." Steve shrank back. "Is it ... is it precious?"

"It's only rose quartz," Cali said, quietly. "But it's not for sale."

There was a long pause. Howard shuffled over. "It's beautiful," he said. "Scary, too."

Another shower had closed in around the cottage. It hissed on the roof and darkened the window, so that the candle warmed the two boys' faces as they leaned in close to look.

The shell case had ripped itself open and gaped like a man-trap, with teeth. In the middle, cradled, was a single pure pink crystal. Howard thought of the crocodile mother he'd seen on a wildlife documentary, holding her wriggling babies safely in her dreadful jaws.

He stopped his hand, just in time, as it reached out to touch. "Sorry," he said, and the candle fluttered with his breath. The light in the quartz, too, shivered like a flame that might go out. Cali did not speak. She was watching, so still that suddenly Steve and Howard were uneasy. "Don't move," she said – too late, because they both looked round. "I didn't touch," said Howard.

"It's all right," she said, turning away. "I was just thinking. Never mind..." She began feeling the wet clothes by the fireside, ignoring the boys.

"What were you thinking?" said Howard.

"I said: never mind. You wouldn't understand." She

turned Steve's jeans inside out with a brisk shake and frowned, just like any mother.

"Can we go now?" said Howard. She shook her head.

It's a trap. What had the man at the Gate, his father, warned him in his dream? *She'll never let you go.*

"We've got to go," said Howard. "Why won't you let us?"

Cali bunched up the jeans and slung them at him. Warm and damp, they hit him like a sweaty animal. "Put them on if you want. Do you really want to go outside in *that*?" The rain was scoring streaks across the grey window. "Did *I* ask you to call? Did I say: do drop by for a nice cup of tea? No, you were off on your big Boys' Own adventure. When it got too much you came scratching at my door. I can do without your problems, thank you. The moment it eases, you can do the manly thing and get your backsides out of here."

11.

"What's the time?" Steve was staring at the window, fidgeting. Howard looked at his watch, and shook it. Nothing. The digital display was as blank grey as the sky outside. He shrugged. The two boys sat paralysed with boredom, like the worst sort of Sunday afternoon. Cali ignored them completely. She was out the back, in the kitchen, getting on. Since the angry, awkward moment with the *Rowan* crystal, they did not dare look at anything too closely, just in case.

Between them and the door, the dog stretched. It yawned all the way to its back teeth. Each time either of them stirred, its sheepdog ears cocked and it watched them with one wary eye. The rain was not clearing. If anything, the day was getting darker, so the walls seemed to draw in closer. Perhaps it was evening already. How long had they been there? There was no clock in this house of stones and bones – a place that no one, maybe, knew was even there.

"We're not going to get back," said Howard. "Mum'll kill me."

"You said: just walk up the hill. Oh yeah... If we'd turned back when I said, we'd be home by now."

"We couldn't have," said Howard. True. From here it seemed so obvious: all that happened *had* to happen, just to lead them here.

Wherever they sat, the goddess in the picture watched them. Her eyes were the only things that did not get darker as the day drew in. Her cloak changed from grey to black and it seemed to fold tighter round the little girl. Like any mother, animal or bird, she was warning them: *one step closer and...*

"I didn't want to come in the first place," said Steve. "I wanted to go down town. It was your idea. You and your crazy stuff about your Gate..."

Howard just sat. Yes, he could say: you're right, it's crazy. But what was the point? As Steve started again, Howard got up and walked to the door of the back room. It seemed to be the only other place to be.

Cali was rinsing something in a stone sink. Howard stood in the doorway behind her, his bare feet prickling on the mat. He had sort of assumed that she would go round barefoot, like hippies did, but a pair of clumpy working boots showed at the hem of her tie-dyed skirt. Even in summer, these stone floors were cold. In winter... Thin as she was, she must be tough.

From this angle, she did not seem strange or frightening at all. She was not much taller than his mum. "Sorry," he said. "It's kind of you to take us in." Cali shrugged and went on rinsing.

"What are you doing?"

"Washing bottles. For the wine."

"You make wine? With those kits from Boots?"

"You can make wine with anything. Dandelions. Cowslips. Birch bark. Anything that's free."

Howard took a breath. "Don't mind my asking," he said. "But... *what* were you thinking, in there?"

She glanced over her shoulder. "You wouldn't want to know."

"Why not?"

"Because you'd be *embarrassed*, that's why. Men can't stand it."

"Oh," said Howard. "I'm used to that."

She turned, wiping her hands on her skirt. "OK," she said, slowly. "I was thinking: there you were, two little boys on your big manly hike, and just for a minute, you forgot all that. There were your faces, just *that* far apart – men never get that close, unless they're fighting. You looked *beautiful*...

"There... I told you you'd be embarrassed. Don't worry, I'm not into little boys. But why's it so dreadful to say it? Steve's got a really *pretty* face. He tries so hard to hide it, all those cool and sneery looks he puts on. And you..." She paused.

"Go on."

"I thought: how will *he* manage? Crab without a shell. You'll have to get yourself some armour somehow. That's what it's all about, isn't it, being a man? Ah, well." She turned back to the bottles on the shelf. "That's why I said: don't move. I thought: why can't they stay like that...?"

She's nothing like Mum, thought Howard, except one thing: she looks tired. Did Mum look like that years ago? Did she go on being tired till she got all hard and grey? "It's OK," he said. "I don't mind."

"Want a taste?" Cali held a bottle up to the light. "Ask Steve."

"Oh, he'll try anything."

They banked up the fire. The wood was furry with lichen that flared up when each log went on. The glasses were chipped and cloudy, but the wine – blackberry, she said – was sharp and clear. It was cold, but it left a warm feeling inside you.

"Would your mothers mind?" said Cali. "Oh well, tell them it's like the brandy the St Bernards take to people lost in the snow. When those clothes are dry enough, I'll run you into Princetown in the van."

"Thanks," Howard mumbled. He tried to remember the Gate, but it was fading, sinking further into mist. Only the slash of the rain on the window now and then said: it's still there...

"Do you go round in the convoys?" Steve said. "With your van?"

"Used to. That's how we found this place. Ten years ago. We came for the solstice – there are stones in the hill, you know, circles, alignments. Then we ... I stayed." There was a pause. A log in the fire hissed. "Unfinished business," she said.

"Don't you get scared, out here alone? Everyone's been telling us stories. The Flip Flop Man. The Hairy Hands..."

Cali smiled. "Poor old Flip Flop – lonely, sneaking thing, with his cold wet fingers. He's just a dirty old man. And there's Childe and his horse."

"I haven't heard that one."

"This hunter, he was riding across the moors one night and he was caught out in the snow – miles from anywhere, no chance of getting back, so what did he do? He took his horse – he was a hunter, remember, the kind of man that kills things for a living – and he cut it open. Then he got inside."

Howard closed his eyes and saw the sheep in the bog with

its belly ripped open, blackened flesh and white ribs showing. Imagine. *Got inside.*

"It was warm, for a while. Then when the horse cooled down and stiffened and Childe knew he was going to die anyway, he wrote his will, with his bloody finger, on a stone. That's the story."

"Poor horse," said Howard.

"Maybe. Or maybe they stayed like that, one spirit, because they died together, one inside the other. Horse-man. Sometimes you see a stallion up there, apart from the rest, and the way it looks at you, you wonder." She poked the fire. "Or maybe you don't."

"And the Hairy Hands?" said Steve. "They aren't sad and lonely."

"Oh, but they are, they are. That's why they're vicious. Fancy, only being hands ... How many men in that prison out there – no, how many men *full stop* – have had that feeling, when their hands go wild? Start doing things their heads don't mean? That's what they say afterwards, anyway."

"But it's only a story," said Howard.

"That's Dartmoor. It's *made* of stories."

"But they aren't true."

"Is Dartmoor true? You've felt what it's like. It soaks things up. Everybody who's lived there, everyone ..." She paused. "Who's died. All the stories and songs. It's like the bog. Once things go in, they last for ever. Who's to say the Flip Flop isn't as real as you or me?"

Rain slashed the window. Howard shivered, though one side of him was scorching, too close to the fire. After a long hush Cali started humming. It was a slow tune, climbing one step up, two steps down, like steady footsteps over rough ground.

"What's that?" said Steve. "You were singing it earlier."

"The Lyke-Wake Dirge. You should know it."

"Who's it by?"

"It's not *by* anyone. It's very old." She sang:

"This ae night, this ae night,
Every night and all,
Fire and fleet and candle-light,
And Christ receive thy soule."

"Sounds like a hymn." Steve wrinkled his nose.

"It's a rite of the dead. A route map to the next world. Don't laugh..." And she slipped from one song smoothly to another:

"There's a way
You gotta find
Out of this world..."

"That's Skeleton Crue!"

"Of course. Where do you think Max stole that song from?"

"You've *met* him? You *know* him? *Madmax? Truly?*"

"I met him at Glastonbury, years ago. I did him a rat's skull, fool's gold in the sockets – it seemed *him*, somehow. Sorry, he's your hero, isn't he?"

"What's he like? I mean, really."

"The trouble with your heavy metal rockers," she said, "is

all they read are horror stories. He thought the Lyke-Wake Dirge needed a bit more action – a few zombies, the odd vampire. Shame." She gave her vixen frown. "The life he lives... He'll need the route map sooner than he thinks."

> *"When thou from hence away are past*
> *Every night and all*
> *To Whinny Moor thou comest at last*
> *And Christ receive thy soule...*
> *But if hose and shoe thou never gave none*
> *The whins shall prick thee to the bare bone..."*

Outside, the rain blew and the whins – gorse bushes – trembled and dripped. Cali stared at the fire as if it was a window that opened into Purgatory, like the song:

> *"If meat and drink thou never gave none*
> *The fire shall burn thee to the bare bone..."*

Steve was watching her, eyes wide. Enchanted. All of a sudden Howard saw how he'd been conned. She'd dropped a name and suddenly Steve loved her. *A trap... She'll never let you go.* He closed his eyes.

Little Howie was lying in bed. Dad was reading him the story of the witch's cave. Dad liked that one best and he read it a lot. Howie found it a little bit scary but he liked it because Howie liked what Dad liked, and he waited for the bit where Dad slowed down and said in a spooky voice, just as they reached the cave: *It's a trap... She'll never let you go.*

Then *Click* – the moment Howie hated when the light went off. Dad was standing in the doorway with the landing light behind him, slowly closing the door. Gone.

"We've got to get back." Howard got up suddenly. Steve blinked and looked up. "Oh... Yeah... OK then." As they struggled into their crisp-baked clothes he said, "Glad you saw sense about the Gate. Not getting there, I mean. I was starting to worry about you..."

"I'll get the van," said Cali.

"I'll come with you," said Steve. "I want to see this."

"Give me a minute," said Howard. "I'll catch up." He thought: *Like heck I will.*

1 2 .

The goat gave him a long indifferent look. *Good girl*, thought Howard. *Don't bleat. Don't rattle that chain.* He fumbled with the gate. It was tied shut with farmer's twine so tight that he couldn't tell which side was meant to be the hinge. Finally he gave up and high-stepped over it. The goat went back to its grass as if this kind of thing was always happening.

Steve's voice drifted up from the outhouse, going all *wow-look-at-that* about the van. Cali said something too and they both laughed. Howard turned and faced into the mist.

That way was up, he was sure. Though the rain had stopped, a thick grey cloud had settled round the cottage. He could see maybe twenty paces, but the ground rose steeply and the mist was darker there. He climbed, holding his breath and watching his feet; the smallest sound would carry. He didn't want that dog of Cali's yapping round his heels. When he turned and looked back, the garden gate was out of sight.

The van gave a cough, whined two or three times and juddered into life. "Get a move on, Howie," Steve's voice called.

"Hey, Howard, we're off!" he shouted, a minute later.

"Howard?" There was not much time. Steve was going back to look.

It should have been easy. After all, they'd been so close. Just out of this dip, and he would be almost at the summit. He'd have done it, he'd have seen it through where Steve had chickened out, he'd show them all. What happened after that would look after itself.

Something was in his way.

The darkness in the mist firmed up suddenly, and became a wall of stones. Great blocks of granite heaped up in a tumbled pile. Sharp overhangs leaned out, with drips of water quivering on their lips.

"Howard?" Steve's voice came from inside the house, then outside again. The door slammed.

Stay calm now. Watch your breathing. Howard skirted the edge of the spoil heap, back the way they had come. It couldn't be that big... The van revved a few times, then stopped.

It was very still around him. Far from coming to an end, the stone tip was nudging further down the slope. It was edging him down. Much further, and it would bring him back on to the track.

"Howard?" Cali's voice was close behind him. She was climbing from the garden gate. Howard thought he heard a panting – the dog's or his own? – in the mist.

This was it. He could turn back, it wasn't too late. He could walk back to meet her and say... what? "Oh, just playing hide-and-seek." Silly Howard, just one of his funny ideas. He needs looking after...

No.

Above him was a gully, full of smaller rocks and chippings. Howard's hands and feet found holes; they were sharp-edged and cold but he was climbing. Then a stone came loose and clattered down the scree.

"Howard? Is that you?" Steve's voice was just beneath him.

The mist was thinning slightly, and there were his head and shoulders, half-way up. "I can see you. Come and get in the van."

Howard did not answer. "Don't be stupid," Steve said. "Cali's going to think you're mad."

"You go back if you want to," said Howard. "I told you I'd get to the Gate and I will."

"Great! Fantastic! What am I supposed to tell your mum?"

"Don't tell her anything. I'll explain when I get back."

Steve was shinning up fast. "Oh, cut it out, this is a stupid game." As he grabbed at Howard's right foot, the left kicked out and caught Steve's knuckle. "Christ! You nutter!"

"I'm not playing. Leave me alone."

"You've cracked. You're nuts. Dunk's got nothing on you." Steve tensed for another grab, but did not make it, one eye on Howard's foot. "That's it. That's where it started, isn't it? Dunk's silly stories. Look, you need help, man. You're coming down with me."

"You can't make me."

" 'Course I can. You're a lump of lard. I'm twice as strong as you."

That's how it had been since the first time they met. Taking care of little Howie – it had been a game for Steve. It made him feel big – bigger than Howard, bigger than the others. And while he did it, Howard shrank and shrank. *Thank you, Steve*, he would say, as he tagged along after him. But Howard wasn't playing any more.

"What are you going to do? Beat me up like the other kids? Knock me unconscious and carry me back?" Steve moved.

Howard raised his foot. Steve shrank. "See who's stronger now..."

Steve made a grab, and missed. The lunge took his foot off its foothold and he slithered, bumping, grating, down the scree. "Idiot! Nutter!" he called, from the bottom. But Howard was gone.

Beyond the rise was a short drop to a quarry track. Left? Right? Left seemed to lead back to the cottage, so he took the right, and ran. His footsteps shuddered back and forth around him in the mist. Echoes. He was in the quarry. Dimly, through the grey, he could make out black rock faces, square-cut and vertical, first on one side, then the other, then ahead.

A trap...

The quarry floor was flooded, so the track led straight into stony-grey water. Round the edge a few thin rushes quivered. Further in, a cairn of rocks poked through; further still, a rusted pulley keeled over sideways; beyond that, mist and ruffled water, no knowing how deep. Howard edged round it gingerly, on small lips of gravel sometimes, sometimes slippy stones.

He heard Cali's voice, and Steve's, together. First they sounded miles away, then suddenly close. They must be in the quarry. "Howard!" they called. In the furthest corner, Howard shrank against the cliff. There was a crack here, just wide enough for a body to squeeze in. He peered up, then braced his back against one wall. With his feet against the other, he could push. He gained an inch. He pushed again; he squirmed.

Cold water dripped down his neck, to his vest. Knobs of granite grated on his spine, his knees... But he was climbing.

Then, when he was two or three times his own height up, he stopped, legs trembling with the effort, as his head grazed something huge and cold. A great wedged block was in his way.

Cali and Steve came to the edge of the water together. The Inland Sea, she called it sometimes, when it was blue with the sky on clear bright days. When it was grey she thought of Tuonela, the lake in the old Northern legend that lay between the land of the living and the land of the dead. There was a piece of music for that too, cold and grand: *The Swan Of Tuonela*. Right now, there was no time for fancy names.

She was angry with these kids, they were wasting her time with their hide-and-seek. Little boys' games... It wasn't till she reached the water, and they'd not found Howard, that she felt the first chill of unease. It wasn't till the great splash echoed round the quarry walls, echoed and echoed, and grey ripples started lapping at her feet, that she was afraid.

13.

"I blame myself, of course."

"You mustn't..."

"But I do." Howard's mother stared straight ahead through Mrs Blundell's windscreen. The head-teacher gave up arguing and drove. Fourth left: Vista Gardens. "I blame myself because I didn't spot the signs," said Howard's mother, as they drew up outside number 23. "It was Steve this, Steve that, *Steve*'s allowed to go to discos, *Steve*'s going to Florida for his holiday..."

"Let's not jump to conclusions," the head-teacher said, as Steve's mother's outline showed through the frosted glass door.

"Come on in, sit down," she said. "I'll put the..."

"Never mind about that. Where has he taken him?"

"What? Who?"

"I think we had better sit down," said Mrs Blundell quietly. Mrs Harris accepted an end of the sofa. She stared holes in the carpet. Down in the deep pile she could see the silt of TV meals.

"Now." Steve's mother brought the tea. "I can't keep calling you Mrs Harris."

"Marion."

"Marion, that's nice. Call me Sue..." *Steve? Dartmoor?* Sue raised her eyebrows. "Hardly. Not the boy-scout type, if you know what I mean." She caught Marion's quivering look.

"Oh, I'm sorry. Shouldn't laugh. You're really worried, aren't you?" That was when Marion burst into tears.

"I knew. I just knew," she muttered.

"Knew *what*?"

Marion looked up. "I knew it would happen. He'd run away. That's what his father did, you know. No warning. No note. Nothing." The crumpled skin around her eyes was grey, like corrugated paper in the ashes of a bonfire. "Doesn't everybody know?"

"No, no. Howard's never talked about his dad. Not a word."

Howard's mother was nodding. "Just like his father," she said, after a while. "He was quiet. A dark horse."

"Poor dear... Do you want to talk about it?"

Marion shook her head. Then she said, "That's where he's gone. To him."

"To him?" the head-teacher put in cautiously. "Are Howard and his father in touch?"

"No! Never. That man's never been mentioned. Not since."

"Well, if Howard doesn't know where he is –"

"He could be looking."

"*You* know, though?" said Susan. Marion nodded.

"Do you think," said Mrs Blundell, "you should speak to him, just to make sure?"

Marion stared straight ahead. "I couldn't," she said. "Never. Never."

Then the phone rang in the hall.

* * *

The splash echoed round the quarry. Whispers of it hung for minutes in the mist.

I can't move, Howard thought. *I'll never move again.*

There had been a chink of light, an opening, where the overhanging boulder blocked his way. If he could just squeeze deeper in the crack he could wriggle through. He got his head in, then his shoulders, then he braced a leg like this...

There was a grinding lurch. Something ripped past, giving his knee a numbing crack as it went. Where there had been stone he was kicking thin air. As he slipped, the rock grated his skin. His arms pushed out by reflex, and he was wedged – wedged tight. He could not turn his head. His heart was banging fit to split his ribs; the cliff shook with it. *I can't move,* he thought. Then his dangling foot found a ledge.

If I ease myself out slightly ... I can breathe.

No! I'm slipping... No, careful. Half an inch... The echoes of the splash still tingled in the mist. *Got to move. Can't breathe.* Little by little, he eased his body out towards the drop.

His other foot found a hold. It was solid. Howard breathed. And looked.

Through the mist beneath him, something dark was moving. Steady, waiting, water slapped the rock beneath his feet. *Don't look down, everybody knows that, don't look down.* He looked up. The mist was swirling there, but paler. The crack was opening and the angle easing, not too far above his head.

If he could dare to leave the foothold, he'd be almost there.

The sound of the splash must have died out by now, but something went on rushing in his head. It was like white-water rapids, but the boulders in it were scraps of words and songs.

Gone too far . . . Gone insane . . . KRRRANG! And Cali's voice, odd antique words he did and didn't understand. *The whins shall prick thee to the bare bone, and . . .* Thud-and-a-Thud-and-a . . . Heartbeat like thunder, or like heavy drums. Don't look down.

He edged his left leg out, up. The numbness was fading and there was a pain in the knee as if someone was prising the kneecap off with a bottle-opener. Push. Yes. Before the pain in the knee got too bad he'd made an inch or two. He wedged himself again and breathed a little. Then he moved, an inch or two, again.

With a rip, the seam of his shirt gave way. A few crumbs of grit that had found their way inside his collar slowly worked their way down his back; they scratched the skin like claws.

The crack was widening. As he climbed, the rock was changing. More cracks, more holds, more edges. Bits of gravel. Getting loose.

It was too wide to wedge himself easily now. His shoulders and thighs were shuddering with the effort, with a steady burning pain. *Don't stop.* He craned his head, blinking the sweat back, and swung out of the chimney straddling it, arms and legs spread like the figure in the Gate. *Don't give up.* Howard swayed. For a moment he thought he would keel out backwards, after all this, and fall and fall. *Face the rock. Don't look down.*

He swayed out, hung just on the point of balance, then swayed back. He closed his eyes. *What if I get breathless? Don't think that. Don't think.* He found a handhold. Moved a foot. He levered up and he was climbing, really climbing. He could do it.

He reached up for a good hold, pulled, and gasped. It didn't come away quite, but it gave a little. Howard froze. He was nearly there, the edge was just above his head and suddenly, to cheat him, the rock was crumbling – not good quarry slabs any more but loose stones and topsoil. He couldn't trust it any more.

Overhead, in the curdling mist, a shape . . . A bush. Knotty stems curled out over the edge. They looked sturdy and thick. Howard's feet were juddering on their small holds and he felt the long drop like a draught up his back. *I can't hold on.*

He grabbed for the bush. As his hand closed round it, one foot slipped. It scrabbled but the hold was gone. Howard's other hand grabbed and somehow there was a scorching pain in both hands as his other foot slipped and the bush sagged with his whole weight.

The bush bent, but did not break. Gorse is tough. His feet kicked like a swimmer's, sometimes making contact, sometimes not, just enough, and his arms were hauling him, hand over hand, with the strength that he didn't have in him, not Howard, not him, and he was crying with the pain that bit deep in his palms, but not out loud, as he thrashed himself over the lip of the quarry, right in the midst of the gorse bush, and he lay there panting and sobbing, as the cold mist settled on his face.

The whins shall prick thee to the bare bone
And Christ receive thy soule . . .

But I'm alive, thought Howard. *I did it. Who'd have thought it?*

Not Mum, not Steve. No one. Even as he winced with the pain, he was grinning. *I made it. Look, everybody, I've won.*

Steve's mother stood in the doorway with a look that made Marion freeze. "Something's happened, hasn't it?"

"It's Stevie. He's in Princetown."

"Is he all right?" said Mrs Blundell.

"He's OK. It's not him..."

"Howard," said Marion, in a flat voice. "It's Howard, isn't it?"

Susan looked at the head-teacher hopelessly, as if to say: Help me out. But she could not. Finally she said, "There's been an accident."

14.

There was no going back. Mist brimmed in the quarry like steam in a cauldron. Howard glanced back down the dank crack and his head swirled. Gorse stabbed him through his trousers as he crawled away from the edge on hands and knees. Only when it was well behind him did he try to trust his feet.

He fell. He staggered up again. Just standing in the springy knee-deep gorse was like tightrope walking. Wincing, he picked the prickles out of his hands and when he looked his palms were smeared with blood. He did not look again. If he clenched his fists hard, it numbed them slightly. In front of him, the ground rose into the mist. He pushed on.

It occurred to him, in an idle sort of way, that he might be cold. He was soaked through his sweater and shirt to his sensible vest, and down through his underpants, down to his socks. There was a stinging sensation all over his skin that might be *cold* – if he could just remember what *cold* was. It all seemed a long way away. He felt fine. All these years, he'd lumbered round in a body that felt a bit too big, too much for him, and that feeling was gone. He felt light.

Wrap up warm now. That was Mum's voice. He'd heard it day after day, till it was part of him, lodged in his head. It was nagging away now but it couldn't touch him, just as if he'd done what he'd so often wanted to do: walk out of the room. He imagined her standing there, scolding the spot he'd been standing on, not even noticing he'd gone. He never did, of course. Instead, he said, "Sorry, Mum" and went into his head. He went to an upstairs room inside him and bolted the door, as the sound of her voice went on and on.

He felt a smile on his face. Don't worry, Mum. If you could see me now . . . I'm doing all the things you told me not to, all those years, and I'm just fine.

He was out of the gorse now, back on open moorland like the slope they'd left, when? Hours or years ago. That was another world. He was sorry that Steve couldn't be here with him for this last bit, but Steve's heart hadn't really been in it. He'd be better off down there by the fireside in Cali's cottage. *A glass of cowslip wine?* said the witch. *Let me sing you to sleep* . . . Was that one of Dad's stories – the gingerbread house? Or one he'd heard at school about Ulysses, where she turned them into pigs?

It's a trap . . . *She'll never let you go* . . . But he'd done it. He'd escaped.

The slope was steep, and he wished that his knee would behave. Every now and then it just buckled under him and he almost fell. It wasn't exactly that his leg was hurting. There was a big lump of something round there that must have been pain, but like the coldness it was miles away. He just wanted the knee to behave.

Behave! That was one of Mum's words. It meant: do what I say. *Did you behave yourself?* What a weird thing to say. Howard said it several times over till the words stopped meaning anything and he chuckled out loud.

Damn. That knee again. He caught himself against a boulder and stayed leaning against it, breathing heavily.

You've got to be careful. What if you had one of your breathless spells? That was his mum's voice again. No, he couldn't go on the trip to Alton Towers. He couldn't go on rides at the fair. What if he had one of his turns? What if his mother wasn't with him? *No,* her voice came from way back. *No, Howard can't come out to play.*

She'll never let you go . . .

Howard's chest was tight now. He was panting, gasping even, but, he thought all of a sudden: *maybe that's what being tired is like?* Maybe everyone got out of breath sometimes? Maybe others just didn't panic and think: *oh, no, one of my turns!*

He looked up. The mist was thinning. Not just the nearest boulders rose up in the grey, but boulders beyond them, and more beyond that. It was still grey, almost like the grey of the evening, round him and behind him, but above, where the summit must be, there was a glow. One last push, and he'd be there, in the light.

Now there was no way round the stones. Sometimes they arranged themselves in steps to help him. He leaned on each knee as he heaved up and that way the pain was less. Sometimes the ground was against him – grit slipped under his feet like a hamster's treadmill. Once he took a long step on to a flat stone that rocked, throwing him sideways, so he whacked his knee again. He crouched for a long time, as small fireworks of pain burst round him in the mist. After that he used all fours like an animal, bending down so low that he smelt the different smells of different stones.

He looked up once. He could see where the slope eased. He climbed for an age, and when he looked it was no closer. He leaned his head on a stone and just for a moment a lovely idea came to him. *I could just lie down.* He could curl up with the mist around him like being tucked up warm in bed. He imagined Mum coming in with a cup of warm milk and some vitamin pills and a little thermometer...

No! The mist ahead was definitely brighter, but he kept his eyes on the ground, planting each foot right and levering, one step at a time. One step and... One step and... One step, and...

Light.

Thirty miles away, the clay hills of Cornwall made a sharp edge with the sky. Above, there were grey clouds, flat as slabs of slate, but the sun had prised them up and pried in under with a long thin shaft of light. Behind him, the low cloud blew across the slope in tatters. Others like it, here and there, dragged over the landscape miles away and far below. There was a distant glint of sea, and Plymouth like a piece of crumpled foil. On the side of the moor each stone and blade of grass was picked out in fabulous detail, painted in with its very own shadow by the slanting orange-golden light.

The sun was just on the horizon. A matter of minutes, and it would be gone. Out of habit he glanced at his wrist – Mum got so upset when he was late – but his watch was gone. There was no time now. The Gate was closer now than ever in his dreams.

It was huge. The two pillars of rock were not the single blocks he had imagined but dizzily balanced slabs as big as cars. One of them leaned as if only the wind kept it up. A gently rising path rolled like a VIP's welcome carpet, right to Howard's feet. All round it there were stones.

They lay embedded in the turf, like beached whales. They

seemed thrown there by a great disaster or an explosion. How silly to think there could have simply been a gate. In the blink of an eye Howard saw the building of which it had been the portal. A stronghold, a fortress, a palace, a prison... He saw how the walls would have shuddered and splintered, starting to slip and slither down the slope. In the midst of it all he saw the tiny figure of a man, arms braced on two pillars, heaving. Not a gatekeeper at all, but Samson, bringing the house down round him.

There was a family, once. Then there was a great crash, but nobody talked about that. In between, there was Dad, with his arms braced ready to heave the pillars of the bedroom door.

Howard hobbled slowly to the ruins of the Gate. There was no one there to meet him. Still, it felt like coming home.

Between the pillars the turf was cropped flat as a lawn. There were hills beyond hills with spotlit patches panning across them. At his feet there was a shallow pool, steel-grey, with fan-shaped ruffles running this way and that. Dartmoor was huge, this was only the edge of it, and for the first time in his little life, thought Howard, he was on his own.

A shudder of movement... Howard saw that he was wrong. He had not noticed the horses, standing patient as rocks, with their backs to the wind, not a stone's throw away. One grey stallion had reared up, long mane whipping, and whinnied. The rest frisked and flared. Then they were thudding away down the slope. He could feel them in the turf as if the moor truly had a heart and it had just begun to beat.

The sun dropped and the west was a deep blush. Howard knew it well. All those times he had crumpled and cringed in front of the class, in front of adults, in shops, on the bus, he had stood there and taken it, like a frightened rabbit, when what he really wanted was to up and run. He should have reared like the wild horses, boxing the air with their hooves, then taken off with the wind.

They were way down the slope already, they were on the next rise, slowing to a canter, then spreading and settling to crop grass again. The darker ones merged with the shadows, but the whitest one, the leader, turned and flounced its mane again.

Cali's cottage, Steve, the bus, school, home, his mum flicked over in Howard's mind like the pages of a book he'd read once, in his childhood, long ago. In that story, the Gate was the end, but now he could see it was just the beginning.

Goodbye, Howard, Howie, Howard the Coward, the odd kid with the silly name and the blush and the body that wouldn't behave. He'd left him behind; someone might find *him* later like a snake's shed skin. He scarcely had to walk; the wind carried him – on through the Gate, to the heart of the moor.

15.

A raven flapped low down the hill, with dog-tired slow beats, towing the night in behind it. Cronk, it said flatly, as if it didn't really care. The last crack of light in the sky was going through the colours of a fading bruise, with the Gate black against it. For the first time Howard saw it behind him. He was inside, looking out.

He was cold. How far he had come he couldn't say, but his left knee had stiffened, and he swayed with each step like a sailor with a wooden leg. Every part of his body said: no. The horses had melted away in the twilight and the hills were closing round him, with no light of a farm or any human habitation. Once an aeroplane passed overhead, miles up, with its wingtips winking and a silvery glow on it from the sun that had long since set down here. The whisper of it came a moment later. Then every human sight or sound was gone.

I'm crying, thought Howard. These are tears on my face, how strange . . . He knew all about crying, how boys didn't do it but he did. It made him ashamed, people laughed, it made him hide his face in his hands. Not here. He could cry if he wanted to, and it seemed he did. That sheep in the bog would have bleated as it went down. When the fox pounced, a rabbit would scream. It seemed strange, from out here, that people made a fuss about it. He did not cry long.

I could die.

It was curious to think that. He said it out loud. It was almost a thrill. Here he was, on the outside of everything, over the edge, with the night coming in. Here was who? Who was Howard? People seemed to think they knew. Mum said: Howard is delicate. Sensitive. Steve's mum said: Polite. The teachers, if they noticed him at all, said: Shy, needs bringing out of himself...

Nobody knew. This was him, on the edge of nowhere. He could die. For the first time ever Howard thought: this is actually me.

He just wanted to sleep.

He wanted shelter. Night was rising like a tide, drowning the valleys, creeping up the slopes. There was a pile of rocks nearby. He dragged himself towards it. It was closer than it looked – the dark did odd things to distances – and a well-worn sheep track led him straight there. Other tracks converged – there was something the animals knew and Howard did not. Then he saw.

Beneath the lip of rock the ground was hollowed to a narrow opening. On hands and knees, he peered in. The tiny cave was empty but smelt warm, of animals. It was out of the wind. The cave felt animal itself, nuzzling round him as he squeezed in. It fitted his body; each lump or groove housed a shoulder or hip. He could feel his heartbeat in the stone.

That's enough, said his body. No more. His eyes closed. Heartbeats, hoofbeats... Sleep, child, they said. Child? he thought. Yes, Childe the Hunter... Cali's story. Why hadn't he seen? It wasn't revolting, it was beautiful. The horse didn't mind. It was part of this moor where things died all the time, died and were taken back and were reborn. He saw the long gash in the horse's belly healing up again, with the man inside it, folding round him and protecting him, poor helpless human, like this rock was folding round him now. He saw the dead horse raise its head and snort. He saw the man's eyes looking at him through its eyes. Cali was right. It was a horseman-spirit, fierce and free.

Inside the ribcage it was warm. Like this. Howard felt a lurch, like falling off the edge of sleep, but he knew it was just the horse flexing its strong legs, rolling over and on to its feet. Now it would rear and flounce its mane. They would be off like the wind. Howard, Childe Howard and the horse. Hoofbeats, heartbeats...

Howard was not stiff or cold or weary. He was galloping.

The moon did not show through the low cloud but the quarry was a blaze of blue-white light. Arc lamps scoured every shadow from the corners and the water shivered in the glare. Beneath the surface, it stayed black.

Men were wading in the shallows, prodding and poking. Some were in up to their waists. They came out shivering, swearing at the cold, and gathered round the sergeant. "Nothing," each reported. "It gets deep," said one. "Another step, I'd have been right off the edge." The last man back had something in his hand. The sergeant held it, dripping, to the light.

"Child's watch," he said. "Strap broken. OK," he said. "That's it. They're bringing the mother out. She'll identify."

Back in the cottage he laid the watch on Cali's table. She looked up from the fire. He concentrated on his lighter, snicking it three times before it lit. He took a long suck on his cigarette.

"Well? Have you found him?" she said. "Tell me."

He did not look at her. "Done all we can do for tonight. Don't want men off with pneumonia." She stared at him. "Look, nobody likes this business," he said. "We'll get a diver in at first light."

"There's no doubt, then," she said.

"Not unless you and the lad are having us on," he said. "Wasting police time?" She met his cold look head on. "No, maybe not. The mother said he couldn't swim."

"The mother... Poor woman."

The sergeant gave a little snort. "Thought you didn't hold with the family, your sort." He looked around the cottage. Hovel, more like. Cheap Indian scarves and hangings drawing-pinned to the walls. A small brass incense-holder with a pile of ash beneath. Probably drugs, if he could be bothered to look. He knew this type. Everywhere they go, there's trouble.

"There'll be questions to be answered," he said.

"I told you. They just turned up at the door. It was raining, so I let them stay. That's all there is to it. Look," she said, "I called you, didn't I? It wasn't just for old times' sake. What do you want me to do?"

"It's not a matter of what I want," he said slowly. "It's the law. I thought we'd moved your lot on years ago."

"There's no one else," she said. "Just me."

"I find that hard to believe. Everyone knows you go about in groups, you ... travellers, or whatever you call yourselves nowadays. Layabouts, more like. Scroungers."

She looked up sharply. The fire behind her caught the

artificial orange of her hair. "There's a boy in that quarry," she spat. "Why don't you think about him?"

He took a last drag on his cigarette, then stubbed it out on the table. "Not a lot we can do for him now," he said. "Strange though... These things seem to happen when you're around, don't they? Coincidence..."

"Get out of my house."

The sergeant raised one eyebrow. "That's another thing," he said. "This cottage belongs to the Morrishtown Quarrying Company. You might think you can just move in anywhere you please, but there's still such a thing as private property in this country."

"It's been empty for twenty-five years. The company's bust. No one'd live here if I didn't."

"Still... A matter of principle. Squatting is a crime. It's the law of the land, and I'm here to see it's respected." The sergeant stepped closer. "I'd move on if I were you."

Cali got to her feet. "This is my home." She looked him in the face. If anything, he was slightly shorter than her. He turned away.

"I don't want anything," she said. "Except to stay here. Just to be here. Dartmoor owes me that."

16.

His hooves made the earth shudder. Sweat was streaming down his flanks but there was no pain any more. Instead of his sore pink scratched chilled skin he had a perfectly-tailored suit of hide. Instead of two weak human legs with their wobbly balance he had four, which flowed with the shape of the hillside, strong and sure.

The hills glowed pale, as if by moonlight, but there was no moon. His night-vision was working, his animal's eyes. The twilight flickered slightly like old black-and-white movies, and he knew with a thrill in his bones that this was not one single night, not just the night when a sad little kid called Howard ran away and got lost. This was the night that had always been there at the heart of the moor.

This ae night, this ae night,
Every night and all...

Night-creatures squealed as he plunged up a hillside, coming to rest at the top. The moor fell away beneath him, and miles down and beyond were the lights of the world.

A village. A town. The gold chain of a bypass, tangled at an intersection. On the horizon, the city under clouds lit by its muddy glow. The human world left orange blotches on the dark, like lichen on a stone.

At the foot of the slope the lights were few and far. They huddled in twos and threes, turning in on themselves, not wanting to look over their shoulder at the dark mass of the moor. There would be dogs at the gate, barbed wire, locked doors.

In between them were fields, hedged with stones. People nibbled away at the edge of the wild. They gained ground slowly, like trench warfare. A farmer would boast about the new field he had made, and his neighbours would envy him, then next year he was hobbled with arthritis or dead of a chill and his neighbours nodded wisely as sheep broke the wall and the field slipped back to being what it always was secretly: part of the moor.

The circles and rows of great stones on the skyline had been there for longer than any of them, like an inscription in a language no one cared to remember. No one in their right mind went there any more. There were mounds, too, and once in a while someone with more nerve than sense broke one open for gold and found bones. Sometimes one struck lucky, finding copper rings and pins that crumbled in his hands, and if he fell from his horse or caught a fever later everyone knew why.

Small tough houses with small-minded tough-hearted people in the shadow of the moor... Nothing changes, everyone who lived here knew, and they didn't like folk who thought it did. Townies come for the day or the week? OK, but woe betide them if they plan to stay.

There was a flicker of light in the blur of years passing. A clutter of brightly painted buses in a lay-by, with a ragged campsite spilling out of them, down to a stream. Some of the tents were just polythene stretched over branches, flapping in the wind like the fertilizer bags that snag on the wire round any farmer's field. He saw a bender ripped from its mooring, cartwheeling off in the wind and people scattering; shadowy figures stepped out from the hedgerows, toting sticks and stones. He saw the windscreen of a purple van smash inwards. People were shouting, and a child shrieked once and then ran.

His horse's nostrils tensed to the smell of burning. He reared and headed for safety, the heart of the moor.

He forded a stream, throwing up a silvery spray in the not-quite-moonlight, and clattered out on a beach of bare stones. The ghosts of the tinners who had lived and died here whispered at him from their scraped-out holes. The ground gave a hollow shiver underfoot, like the pumping of mining engines in deep shafts, going down for the copper and tin. Those underground chambers were empty again. At the end of the seams, in the absolute darkness, no one would strike a light or a pick-blow to disturb the sleep of crystals in the rock. White teeth of quartz. Fool's gold.

There were bangs and shudders round him; men were attacking the moor. His horse's hide bristled at the thump of blasting in the quarries: a hollow crump, then a throat-rattling slither of rubble. Then there was another flash and thump, flash and thump at carefully timed intervals, as men played at being gods of thunder, firing broadsides at the wilderness, practising for war.

He came to a flat stretch, quiet now, where the ground was dark and soft. There were pools of open water, and a murmur where a stream began to gather. Up the track beside it came a child, too young to be out alone. She had been running; her long hair was tangled and the hem of her dress was muddy and torn. She was not crying any more. She was wandering, slightly dazed but not afraid of this place, as if she knew, whatever had scared her, that she would be all right here.

She sat on a tuft and looked round. Better wait. She couldn't see Mummy coming but she would soon. This was their favourite place, where they came when there was any trouble. Soon Mummy would come and find her here.

The girl hummed for a while, no particular tune. Then she talked to the horse that was cropping the grass on the other side of the pool. She tossed a knot of grass into the pool and watched the wind sail it. Then, in the dark clear water, something caught her eye. A silvery thing, with a round end and a circle on it, almost buried in the soft peat. Treasure! She crouched at the edge and, wincing at first because the water was so cold, reached in to claim it.

To the horse's quick reactions, the pool seemed to rise in a silvery spray. The shock in the air made him shrill out in terror, and he laid his ears back and went thudding away. Across the flat and up the slope, he galloped, slowing only when he was out of sight of the bad human thing that had happened back there.

The horse stood facing the wind, looking down on a new view. It was already forgetting what had happened. Things died: that was the way of the moor. Even the peat they walked on was the death of centuries of moss. But that was a child. For the first time on his night ride, Howard's human eyes looked out and could not see, *would* not see just what the horse saw: a minute of panic, then things going on. That was a child, thought Howard's human mind. One moment, a human child, just inquisitive, playing... The next, no sign of life except a couple of crows, alarmed by the explosion, flapping away. But the horse's mind had moved on.

That was the village down there. This one was not like the others, not huddled for shelter with its clutch of farms, but built on the brow of the moor. Two roads met and there were houses, but out to one side were two blocks so huge they seemed more like outcrops than buildings. Each had row on row of windows, very small. Around the perimeter, there was a high wall; where it met the road there was the massive granite gate.

One day, not many years back, just a blink of an eye in the life of the moor, there was a small car driving on the road to Princetown. The mother and the father in the front were not speaking, just staring out blankly, and the small boy in the back seat stared out too. He never knew what he was supposed to do. Mum kept on saying Dad should take them for an outing, and when at last he said "All right, get in the car" it seemed to be better for a while because they didn't argue. They didn't say anything at all, and after a while that was worse.

"What's that place?" said little Howard.

"That's the prison," said his mother. "See the great big gate?"

"What's it for?" said Howard.

"That's where they put men when they're bad. They lock them in."

The boy pressed his nose to the window. "Only men?"

There was a pause. Dad wasn't saying anything, but then he had to drive. "Yes," said Mum. "Only men are that bad."

"What do they do to the bad men?" the boy said some minutes later. "Do they smack them?"

"No," said his mum. "They make them break up stones."

"Why break up stones?"

"No reason. Just because they're bad. It takes a long time."

Little Howard had to think, so nobody talked any more. On their way back they passed a little quarry in the hillside; that must be where the bad men went. There were piles of the stones already. *How small do they have to break them?* he thought, and he closed his eyes and saw a huge grey beach. All the hills had been broken into gravel, which stretched on as far as he could see, and in the middle of it bad men stood and looked at each other. *What do we do now?* they said.

The horse on the hillside frisked its skin as if a fly was biting. *That was Mum and Dad,* said Howard. *That was me.*

The horse pawed the ground with a forefoot. *You don't want to be him again,* it seemed to say. *You managed to forget it once. Forget again.*

When the car had pulled in for petrol at the Daws Cross garage, Mum told little Howard to get out and stretch his legs. He climbed a low hedge and gazed at the moors. "Look," he said, pointing at the two bumps on the skyline. "Is that where the bad men go?"

"Don't listen to your mother," said his father. "I don't."

"What did you say?" His mum had come up quietly behind them. "Howard, go and wait in the car." Even with the windows wound up tight he could still hear them shouting. He covered his ears.

Not long after that Dad didn't come home. "Why has Daddy gone away?" Howard said.

"Your father was a bad man," said Mum. "That's all there is to it. And I don't want you to talk about it any more."

It was cold on the hillside. Howard was sitting on a rock, looking down at the prison. There it was, the gate. He shivered. The stallion was gone, and he was back with his two weak legs and thin skin, no warm hide to wrap around him any more. Just for a moment he thought he was quite alone.

A hand clamped on his shoulder. "Well, what in all damnation's this?" a voice gruffed. "Bog knows," said another, thin and nasal. It sniffed wetly. "Skinned rabbit, looks like." A hand slapped on his other shoulder. Both were damp – one sweaty-hot, one dripping cold. "Well, boy, what you got to say?"

17.

The man stepped into the room. All these years Cali had bolted the door each evening, keeping the dark out. This one night, because it would be her last, she had left it open. The room was stripped of its curtains and hangings, and she had packed her tools and books and stones. The place was bare again, the way she had found it ten years ago. Only the charcoal drawing of the Goddess was left above the embers of the fire. She belonged. Let someone else meet her one day, when Cali was gone.

And tonight of all nights a man had to walk in.

"Oh... I'm sorry," he said. "I thought the place was empty. Then I saw the candle..."

He was big. He had to stoop a little from the roof beams and his wide coat looked well filled. His round pink cheeks were flushed in the candlelight. A cheerful face, it might have been, but not now.

"Like I said... I'm sorry. If I'd have known... They didn't tell me..." He backed to the door. "You see, it's my boy..."

"*Your* boy? Howard?" Cali uncrossed her legs – they were stiff from hours of sitting – and came up to a crouch. The quiet of the night was ruined anyway – as usual, by a man. But this one looked lost and sheepish. "Howard's friend told me he didn't have a father."

The man looked at the floor. "Yes, well..." he said, and blushed. "In a way."

"You'd better sit down," said Cali.

"I got the call around midnight," he went on. He did not check if she was listening. "Anne-Marie picked it up and she said: it's the police, they want to speak to *you*. What's going on? she said, I don't like this. Then they told me..." His hands were dangling between his knees. He looked like a kicked dog. "They said there was no point coming till first light, but I couldn't just lie there. In the end Anne-Marie said, for God's sake go over there if you can't settle, so I did. I thought, if I came... I might be able to do something." He trailed off. Half an hour, thought Cali, and it'll be light. The police will be back. We want you out of here, they'd said.

"You see, I havn't seen him, not for, oh, nearly ten years. Not that I wouldn't have, I'd have liked to but, you know how it is..." He looked at Cali, pleading. Make it all right, said his eyes. She did not.

"Were you here?" he tried again. "When ... when it happened?"

"No one knows what happened," she said. "I heard. I didn't see."

"You mean, there's a chance. He might not have drowned. He could have swum to safety..."

"Could he swim?" said Cali.

"I don't know." There was a long pause. The embers of the last fire in the fireplace crumbled with a little hiss. "You probably think I'm crazy," he said. "Clutching at straws. It's just, I can't, I mean you *can't* believe he's just..." He shook his head.

"I know," said Cali. "Believe me, I do." If the man heard, he gave no indication. He gave a little hopeless laugh.

"I keep thinking," he said, "I know it's stupid but I keep on thinking: like his old man . . . That's what I wanted to do, you see. Disappear. Leave the old life, start over again. I don't know if they told you – no, of course they didn't – but I . . . I left Howard's mother. I was travelling a lot, you understand, and then I met Anne-Marie, well, you can imagine . . ."

"I can imagine," said Cali.

There was a lot more, and Cali heard some of it as she watched the light grow at the window. How Anne-Marie had been such fun to be with but Marion was always nagging, she was like that. How a clean break had seemed better for the child. How the strange thing was that these days Anne-Marie seemed to be going on at him just like Marion used to, always worrying but maybe that was just how women were, sorry, present company excepted. He sighed. "It's a funny old life, isn't it?"

Cali had been lacing her boots. She stood up. "No," she said.

"Are you going to the quarry? I'll come with you."

"No, I'm not. You stay here. The police will be here any minute. Probably Howard's mother too. You'll have someone to talk to." He looked up at her, puzzled. "You just reminded me," she said. "There's somewhere I must go. Alone."

Once, at the zoo, Howard had peered into a glass tank, looking for the Bird-eating Spider. He had pressed his nose to the glass and he still couldn't see it . . . then he had screamed: it was there, an inch from him, so big he had not noticed, as big as his head. The two hands – one hairy and horny, one clammy and pale – were crouched on Howard's shoulders just like that. This time he would not scream.

Howard turned slowly to face the owners of the voices, but he could not look at both, they were too close. They *had* faces, yes, but he could not focus on them. It was the hands he had to watch... That, and the way the strangers sat and moved. One was massive, all chin; he thrust his thick neck forwards like a longhorned bull. The other looked sickly as a plant sprouted under a stone. He seemed like something soaked too long in water. When he moved, he oozed.

"Not to be afraid." There was a damp smell round the thin one. "Won't hurt, will we, Handy?"

If hands can grin, that was what the hairy hands did. "Naaah. Lad's one of us, now."

Howard swallowed. "And who ... who are you?"

The two looked, one to the other. "Don't tell us you don't know." For a moment he thought they were both dressed in baggy pyjamas with arrows on them, like comic-book convicts. The big one guffawed, deep in his chest. The small one smacked his lips – a nasty wet sound, flip, flop...

"I'm Howard. Howard Harris. I'm not one of you."

"Hhhhhoward Hhhhharris, hhheh?"

Howard flushed. He had never been able to say his name out loud without blushing. "It's not funny! I can't help what I'm called."

"Getting riled, eh? Want to hit me, do you, hit yer uncle Handy? Eh? Just like you wanted to hit the others – only those hands of yours, those pale little hands, they didn't dare?"

One of the Hairy Hands came up an inch from Howard's nose. It clenched its fingers, very slowly, as if crunching an invisible aluminium can. "Yer wouldn't dre-e-eam of it, would yer?" The man had a laugh like shovelling gravel.

"Stick with yer Unk, he'll show you how." The two hands came together in a strangling movement. Howard flinched, but the other man's cold breath was in his ear.

"Now, you're going to say: it's not fair. The poor innocent prey! It does you credit, good boy. But it's *not* fair, is it? Was it fair what they did to you? In the playground? Even your so-called *friend*...? Not to mention your mummy and daddy... No, *not* fair. And you were such a good boy." The Flip Flop Man's fingers were long, with wide crinkly pads, like when you've stayed in the bath too long. Where they touched, they stuck. "You have to pass it on, you see. It comes out even in the end."

"Buck up, lad!" said the Hands, in a voice like Mr Fairbairn's. "It's a man's life out here. Can't afford to get soft."

"A lonely life..." The old one's fingers sucked round his arm. "That's why you need *friends*..."

Howard wrenched himself sideways. He could hardly move, something cold and hard held him as if he was wedged between stones. Something jarred his knee; something jabbed in his back. "I don't belong here," he said. "Let me go!"

"But we aren't touching you..." They held their hands up like boys caught stealing: honest, officer... Hairy hands... Frog-foot fingers... Howard twisted again, and his head struck overhanging rock. He blinked, and when he opened his eyes again, he was half in, half out, of the dark of the cave. He squirmed for the entrance.

"One thing," said the voice of the Flip Flop, fading. "Before you try to *leave* us. Are you sure you're here at all?"

A feeling as cold as the Flip Flop's fingers ran down Howard's spine. "Think... In the quarry, could you *really* climb that rock face? You? And aren't you wet and cold? And you can't breathe too easily, can you?" It was very faint now, but it chuckled like a bog stream.

"Don't they say a man's life passes before his eyes – think on it, lad – when he drowns?"

18.

This can't be real...

Howard rolled out of the cave, and blinked his eyes again. On the lip of the overhang, a drip of water wobbled. It wobbled and wobbled and would not drop. A panicky thought came to him, that it might hang there for ever. Maybe time did not pass here. He willed it: drop, *drop*. It did not.

There was light. If it was, if it truly was morning, then he must have slept. He felt as if he had walked a hundred miles. He levered himself up. His elbow twinged. His spine was a necklace of bruises threaded on an ache.

Around him the world was a blank page. No shapes, no outlines. Everything was white.

Yesterday the mist had swirled and eddied. Now it stood, thick and still, a few feet from his face. He got to his feet and staggered a few paces. When he turned back, the rocks were gone. There was no way of telling which way led into the moors and which back.

The only thing that felt real was his thirst. His mouth was sour and sticky. He sucked the cool air through his lips, closed his eyes and thought about a kitchen tap. A glass of water. Yes... He could fool the thirst for a moment. It was angrier when it came back.

Downhill, he thought. If there's water, it will be downhill, and he followed the lie of the land. After a moment there was a sound – a faint ding-dong of running water – in the mist. He dragged towards it, listening every few paces. It was twice as far as it had sounded, and still it seemed no nearer, but where else was there to go but on? Once he thought he heard voices but could not judge where. He tried to call but no sound came from his parched throat. Next time he listened, the voices were gone. He had only caught a snatch, but there had been something familiar about them. *It's all in my mind*, he thought. It couldn't be real.

The water was clearer now, high and tinny like Steve's headphones. Skeleton Crue. *Out of this world*... He found himself singing. *Out of your mind*...

He almost fell into the stream. At first he could not see it even then, with the long grass and moss bent over it. He slurped up handful after handful. He thought of the sheep in the bog, but didn't care. Then he looked up.

The mist was standing further off now, revealing the lie of the land. It was a shallow dip, laced with bog pools and cotton grass. It was like...

Howard shuddered. He had been here before, but he couldn't have. Be sensible... He'd had this feeling before when he was ill or tired; they called it *déjà vu*. And yet he knew there would be a path beside the stream, and when he looked it was there. That was when he felt the footsteps. Something formed in the mist.

It was two-legged, almost human. Its head, if that was what it was, hung down between its shoulders, thrust forwards by the huge hump of its back. Its skin hung in loose folds and patches. It clanked slightly. Just across the stream it saw him.

"Friggin' hell," it said. "What're *you* doing here?"

Private Cameron's face was blacked up like an old-fashioned minstrel. In the panda-like eye-holes, going smeary with dark sweat, his eyebrows crinkled in a frown. "Which way did they go?" he said.

"Go? Who?"

"The rest of the patrol, idjit. They were coming this way. You must have seen them."

Howard felt a sort of swirling in his head. He was being rescued, wasn't he? "Ach, forget it," spat Cameron. "Wee barmpot. I'll find them myself."

"Help me!" said Howard. "I'm lost."

"*You're* lost? *I'm* the one who's lost. The sarge'll have my bollocks. Just tell me, yes or no. Have you seen them?"

"No," said Howard feebly. "I mean, I think I might have heard them. Over that way."

Cameron looked where Howard pointed out across the bog. He came up close. Howard could smell Marmite on his breath. "You sure?"

"Yes... No... I don't know. I think so."

"Well, you'd friggin' well better be right." The soldier turned, his boot grinding a twist in the mud, and thudded away.

"Wait!" said Howard. "You can't just leave me."

At ten paces, Cameron whipped round. Already the mist was thickening between them. Howard could not see his face. He was a figure through a shower curtain or frosted glass.

"Get this, kid. This isn't a Sunday stroll, you know. This is manoeuvres. I can't just stroll down that path and home to Mummy. This is the real thing." He turned his bulging rucksack on Howard and slogged off. The shapes of grass tussocks and pools closed round him in the mist.

Dark water. Howard had seen it. Something glinting...

"No!" Howard called. "Don't go." Cameron did not turn. "No!" shouted Howard. "Not that way..." Cameron was gone. He had left him. "All right!" Howard yelled. "Get yourself killed. I don't care."

The sound of the boots hung in the mist long after the man. He was rushing, you could hear that, getting clumsy in his hurry. Sometimes the footsteps stumbled, and there was a small curse, or they splashed through water. Flip, flop...

Then there was quietness. Then a *whump!* like a punch in the stomach. A long moment later, there was a quiet, almost casual, spattering of falling mud. It must have been buried deep in the soft peat, underwater, the thing with its round shiny end just showing, if you paused to look – the unexploded shell.

Then there was a hush, with just the tinny grating sound of water, and the man's voice in the mist. He was not calling for help; he was not roaring with pain. He seemed to be crying like a little child.

You wouldn't dream of it, the Hands had said. You felt like hurting people when they hurt you, but you didn't care.

This has got to be a dream, thought Howard. *I'll close my eyes and wake up, please. This can't be real.*

There was another movement, on the path behind him. As he turned, the figure stopped. It clutched its long grey cloak tight around it. Cali, with her ember-coloured hair...

"You!" she said. Then, more quietly: "But you're dead."

"I'm not, I'm not. Believe me. Here, touch me." Cali did not move. "I climbed out of the quarry," he went on. "I got to the Gate. I slept in a cave, and, and I'm hungry." She was very still, staring. "And my leg hurts. There, it wouldn't hurt, would it, if I was dead? Say something!"

"You..." she said again. "I heard the explosion and I thought ... I thought I might see *her*."

The mist was suddenly cold round Howard. This place. Of course, he had been here. The small girl with her muddy hemline. With her treasure ... But that was a dream. It wasn't real, or if it was real, it was not *now*.

"That's not her," he said. "That's a soldier. He's really hurt."

The crying in the mist had fallen to a long moan. "Help me ... FerChrissake, someone ..."

Cali stepped right up to Howard. Cautiously she reached a hand out from the cloak and touched ... first his shoulder, then his forehead. "God," she said. "You're freezing. Here ..." She opened the cloak and folded him into its warmth. One arm came round his back and held him close, and for some reason he found himself sobbing. When he took a breath, he felt her sobbing slightly too.

"Let's get you home," she said.

"Hold on ... What about *him*?"

She pulled herself away from him. The grey cape flared out with the sudden movement and her face, turned towards the crying in the mist, was strange and hard. He had seen that face before, once: not the Cali who brought camomile tea, not even the Cali who spat out her anger at *boys' adventures* ... It was the charcoal goddess on the fireplace, but without her child to hold.

"It's just a soldier," she said coldly. "Playing soldiers' games."

"He's injured," said Howard. "Listen!"

Terribly, she smiled. She turned to face him. "So there's such a thing as justice after all."

19.

"Help me... I can't move... Jesus, help me!" The soldier's voice was fainter now, but shriller, in the mist. Howard turned to go towards it – tried to turn, but Cali's eyes were on him. Like a rabbit in the headlights of a car, or in a fox's stare, he could not move.

"We've got to help him," Howard said. "It's not his fault."

"What do you know about it?" said Cali. "They killed my daughter – every one of them. They're soldiers. Soldiers take orders, that's what you join up for, isn't it? No need to think. Sign up and you've signed up for everything the army's done. Every rubber bullet, every drop of tear gas, every shell. Soldiers don't think anything's their *fault*. You sound like one of them."

"No," said Howard. "No. It was my fault. I told him to go that way. And I knew..."

She shook her head, and the hair flounced out a moment like a horse's mane. "Ten years," she said. "Ten years I've waited here for something. Prayed for it. I didn't know what it would be ... but this is it." She smiled again. "It feels good to me."

"They didn't kill her. She found an unexploded shell. I saw."

"*Their* shell. *Their* army. *Their* pathetic war games..." She stopped. "What do you mean: you saw?" His head was swirling again, with specks of brightness in the mist. He could not stand her gaze, but could not take his eyes away. His knees gave way; he crumpled, still looking up, at her feet.

"*You* saw her? You?" There was a catch in her voice, like a splinter. "Ten years I've been coming here. I've never seen her. Felt her, maybe. Never *seen*. Why should she show herself to *you?*"

"I ... I don't know. It was only a dream, I think. But if I hadn't seen her, I could have wandered in there. That could have been me."

The crying, that had ebbed, burst out again. "Christ, I'm sinking. Help me!"

"Come with me," said Cali.

"No!" With an effort, Howard turned his eyes away. He could move. He heaved himself up and pain went through him, but he stood. With Cali's look cold on his back, he limped towards the voice.

"Leave him," Cali called. "She meant him to die. It's her revenge."

Howard looked back – at her feet, not in her eyes. "I don't think she would want that," he said. "She was playing. She was just a little girl."

"Who's that?" Cameron's voice was almost underneath him. Howard could have walked straight past, there was so little of him showing – just the head and one arm clutching a tussock of grass. The rest was in the water. "Quick," gasped the man. "Oh, God, my foot, I think it's gone." The movement was too much; he winced and slipped back further. The water oozed up round his neck. Then Howard had him by the arm.

There was nothing to get a firm grip on. The sleeve of the

combat jacket was slimy and waterlogged; the arm was slipping down inside it, as if something in the pool had hold of the
man and was pulling.

"Jesus," Cameron whispered. His face was turned up, just
a mask shape showing. So close, Howard could see little
craters of acne showing through the black. "Don't let me
drown."

Howard braced his one good foot against a tussock. It gave.
He slipped, he grabbed the arm again, it jerked away and
Cameron went down.

Then Cali was beside him, hauling on the arm. The head
bobbed up again. "Got to get the pack off him," she said,
fumbling in the water, and there was a jerk. She must have
found the buckle, because suddenly the weight eased. The
man's other arm broke the surface. "And the other," she said.
With a jolt, he came free. After that, it was pulling together,
slipping and pulling again, till Cameron's head and shoulders
were on dry land. His two arms hugged round a tussock, like a
child hugs its mother, and he gasped and gasped and could
not speak.

"Cameron? Where are you, man?" One voice, two, three
voices, in the air behind them, and there were the soldiers,
spaced out, combing through the mist. Just for a moment the
five of them stopped and stared at the huddle they could not
quite make out, then they were in action, elbowing Cali and
Howard aside. "You don't have to look," said the Welsh man
as Cameron's legs draggled out of the water. Cali did not
blink or flinch, but Howard looked away.

A few minutes later, a soldier came over to the rock where
Cali and Howard sat. Howard recognized him – the only one

whose blinking patches round his eyes were brown, not pink. "Like, I'm sorry you had to see that, maan," he said. "But thanks. Looks like you saved his life." Cali looked straight back at him and did not smile.

"They've been on the short-wave," he said. "Orders are to wait here. Civilians included. There's a helicopter on its way."

Howard looked round. "The mist's going to lift," said the soldier. It was true. Above them the white had a pale bluish tinge. "Might take a while, but it's better than trying to move him. Hey, boy," he said, shaking his head. "You look wiped out. Don't worry now. You're gonna get a lift home."

When he had gone, Cali spoke. "It would have been so right," she said. "A sacrifice. You know how they find bodies in peat bogs sometimes, from the Iron Age? Offerings to the Goddess, with their throats cut, usually, or strangled. It's what they did with criminals." Howard opened his mouth to speak, but Cali laid an arm across his shoulder. "OK, don't say it. He wasn't a criminal. Just a grown-up kid like you." She was quiet for a moment. "She really was happy, was she, when you saw her?"

Howard nodded. So did Cali, and for a long time neither spoke. "I . . . I've got to ask," he said at last. "You don't have to say. Where were you when . . . when it happened?"

"They broke up our camp," she said. "Some farmers, and men from the village just in it for a laugh. They went at the buses with crowbars. The local policeman – he's a sergeant now, would you believe? – looked on. One of them grabbed me, so I shouted to Rowan to run. I knew she'd make for here.

It was our special stream. Whenever there was any hassle, we'd come here together and sit."

"So," Howard said after a while. "You weren't looking for me?"

"Not you. I was coming to say goodbye."

There was a sudden thudding in the air. As the last shreds of mist began to sunder, the helicopter panned over once and circled, looking for a place to land.

"By the way," said Cali. "I saw your father."

"You can't have. He's in prison."

Cali stared at Howard. "Whoever told you that?"

"No one... I worked it out for myself."

She shook her head. "You thought that? All those years, you thought he was ... a murderer or something, if he was in Dartmoor. Is that what you thought?"

Howard looked down at his feet and blushed. She gave him a squeeze. "Poor kid... He's a travelling salesman," she said. "Sells picture postcards to the tourist shops. It's true... Disappointed, are you?"

"Then ... then why did he leave?"

"You really want to know?" Howard nodded. "OK," she said. "He met a woman in Totnes. Nothing out of the ordinary. Men do it all the time." She rested both hands on his shoulders, till he met her eyes. Then she smiled.

"Poor boy. You don't want to know all this, do you? Never mind. He's not a bad man, your dad, not as men go. I expect he thought he was going on a big adventure."

20.

The pool in the quarry went from grey to blue, just like that. Let your eyes go out of focus, and with the cliff behind you could be looking at an Alpine lake.

The frogman waded out of the shallows, glistening. He hinged off his mask. "Well," the sergeant said.

"Not a sign. Just a lot of rocks down there, and a few bones. Nothing recent."

"Bones? What kind of bones?"

"Bits of sheep, I'd say. Oh, most of a horse."

The sergeant turned away. That was it. Someone was going to get it. Up for Wasting Police Time. He would see to it personally. Tyres crunched on the track at the quarry entrance. WPC Wren came at a trot.

"Message for you, sir. The boy's safe. Some squaddies found him up there on the moor."

The sergeant took a deep breath, through clenched teeth. It would be all over the *Evening Herald*, he could see it. Army finds lost boy. Police search fails.

"Pardon me, sir," said the WPC after a decent interval. "Shall I inform the parents, or will you?"

The sergeant shuddered. He had spent a few minutes in the cottage earlier. He had brought the mother, and they found the father there. He thought of those few minutes. Talk about icy. He'd rather swim in the lake.

"I think, considering all the circumstances, a woman's

touch..." he said. "Just get rid of them, will you? Then we can all go home."

"Why?" Howard shouted, over the rub-a-dub-dub of the rotor blades. Two men were reaching down to hoist him in, but Cali would not budge. He held on to her hand. "Why won't you come?"

She pulled her hand away. "They might give me a medal or something," she said and, for the first time he had seen, she laughed.

"Give Steve my love," she yelled, as his feet left the ground. "And tell him not to waste his time on heroes. Tell him... Tell him Madmax is going bald. Spends a fortune on hair restorer. And..." She hollered. "Tell him to look me up if ever he makes Glastonbury. You too!"

"Me?" mouthed Howard. "Mum wouldn't let me."

Cali laughed. "She's probably right." She came up level with his feet. "Be kind to her," she said, softly. "You can spend a lifetime holding on to something – especially if it hurts. She'll know what I mean. Now..." She slapped the helicopter like a stallion. "Get on with it. Tell them you're a hero!"

She ducked under the shockwaves of the rotor, straightened up again at a distance and waved. Just for a moment Howard balanced in the hatch, arms braced on either side, in a posture he might have recognized if he had been outside to see it, but he wasn't: it was him. Then the whirlybird lurched and strong hands eased him back and sat him upright on the floor. He was briefly surprised to find that the thing inside was just a crate of metal, like being hoisted in a skip. Then everything hammered like the spin cycle starting up in a washing machine. The whole world tilted like a fairground ride.

"Can I look down?" said Howard in a moment. One of the men who had helped him in grinned. "First time up?" he said. "I suppose this is all a big adventure for you?" Howard nodded. It would have been much too complicated to explain.

They came around the moor's edge in a long sweep. He caught sight of Cali way beneath him, and he waved through the hatch but there was no sign that she saw. The dog, whose name he had never even asked, was a grey speck winking through the bracken, tracing wider and wider circles round its mistress. Just for the blink of an eye Howard imagined that there might have been a second smaller figure walking right beside her, then he saw it was only her shadow. He wished his mum could see this woman striding out across the moor alone. He would try to tell her, though he could not think how.

The hill slipped out beneath them, smooth as that trick where you whip the tablecloth away from underneath a glass of wine so quick it doesn't spill. There was a road, but he could not spot the quarry or the cottage or the tor he and Steve had climbed together. He tried to pinpoint which of the thousand cluttered bits of rock was Staddle Tor, but the whole thing was flat as a map. There was no sign where he had struggled or rested or triumphed or given up hope.

It all looked different from here.

Then the helicopter banked and the view from the hatch panned out over the fields of the valley, moss-like clumps of woods and crumbs of villages, out towards Cornwall, where a bright glimpse of the river Tamar curled among small hills on its way from the moors to Plymouth, past the dockyard and the ships at anchor, out to the gleam on the horizon of the open sea.

Philip Gross is a well-known poet, for adults and children, as well as a writer of stories and plays. He grew up in Plymouth and spent many weekends in his teens walking and climbing on Dartmoor. He lives in Bristol now, but still goes back.